FOGGERTY'S FAIRY

AN ENTIRELY ORIGINAL

FAIRY FARCE IN THREE ACTS

Foggerty's Fairy

An Entirely Original Fairy Farce in Three Acts

W.S. GILBERT

with notes and an introduction by

Andrew Crowther

SECRETARY OF THE

W.S. GILBERT SOCIETY

RENARD PRESS

RENARD PRESS LTD

124 City Road
London EC1V 2NX
United Kingdom
info@renardpress.com
020 8050 2928

www.renardpress.com

Foggerty's Fairy first published in *Original Plays: Third Series* in 1895
This edition first published by Renard Press Ltd in 2022

Edited text © Renard Press Ltd, 2022
Introduction and Notes © Andrew Crowther, 2022

Cover design by Will Dady

ISBN: 978-1-913724-74-0

Renard Press is proud to be a climate positive publisher, removing more carbon from the air than we emit and planting a small forest. For more information see renardpress.com/eco.

CONTENTS

W.S. GILBERT

A Brief Introduction

William Schwenck Gilbert was born in London
on the 18th of November 1836. He was educated
at the Western Grammar School, Brompton, and
King's College, London. He had intended to go on
to complete his education at Oxford, but in the event
he was not able to do so, probably for financial reasons.
From 1857 to 1862 he was employed by the Education
Office as an Assistant Clerk (Third Class) – a job he
hated – and he also practised as a barrister between
1863 and about 1867, without much success. He
married Lucy Agnes Turner in 1867, their marriage
lasting for the rest of his life.

In 1861, a new comic journal called *Fun* appeared,
founded in direct imitation of *Punch*. Gilbert began
contributing to *Fun* shortly after its first appearance,
and for ten years he was one of its most prolific con-
tributors, providing whimsical and comic material of
various sorts, including jokes, cartoons, satirical squibs,
parody reviews, stories and comic poems. His riotously

funny *Bab Ballads*, for a long time considered classic, were first published in *Fun*.

However, his ambition was always to write for the stage. His first acknowledged play, a burlesque called *Dulcamara, or, The Little Duck and the Great Quack*, was a great success when it was produced in 1866. He quickly made a name for himself as a bold and original voice in the theatre, writing all kinds of plays from burlesques and farces to serious dramas. In 1872, an article in *The Era* praised him on the grounds that 'more than all others in our day, he has given us… plays which add to our wealth of dramatic literature; plays which must live.'

In 1871, at the behest of theatrical manager John Hollingshead, Gilbert wrote the libretto for *Thespis*, his first collaboration with composer Arthur Sullivan. It was an ephemeral Christmas entertainment, not expected to have a life beyond its first production, and it was received as such. It was the success of their second comic opera, *Trial by Jury* (1875), that led impresario Richard D'Oyly Carte to consider the commercial possibilities of a longer-term collaboration of Gilbert with Sullivan. Two years later, D'Oyly Carte formed an opera company which, over the next twelve years, would produce ten Gilbert and Sullivan operas, including *HMS Pinafore, The Pirates of Penzance, Iolanthe, The Mikado, The Yeomen of the Guard* and *The Gondoliers*. During this time, Gilbert's focus turned more and more towards the Sullivan operas and away from other work.

Over the years, Gilbert's relationship with Sullivan became increasingly strained, due partly to Gilbert's own abrasive personality, and partly to Sullivan's desire to focus on more serious work. In 1890, an explosive business row between Gilbert, D'Oyly Carte and Sullivan fractured the collaboration, though this was later uneasily patched up, leading to two further operas in 1893 and 1896, *Utopia Limited* and *The Grand Duke*.

In 1890 Gilbert moved from his house in Harrington Gardens, South Kensington, to Grim's Dyke, a large country house at Harrow Weald, where he lived for the remainder of his life. In 1897 he went into semi-retirement from the stage, while occasionally writing further plays when the mood came over him. In 1907 he became the first person to be knighted for his achievements as a dramatic author. He died on the 29th of May 1911, suffering from heart failure, having dived into a lake in the grounds of Grim's Dyke, trying to come to the assistance of a young woman who had got into difficulties and called for help.

ANDREW CROWTHER

INTRODUCTION

FOGGERTY: There's one question I should like to ask
– this is not a pantomime?

REBECCA: Bless the man, no.

FOGGERTY: It won't end in my being changed into
Harlequin, and Jenny into Columbine, or any
nonsense of that sort, will it? Because if it does—

REBECCA: You need not alarm yourself. This is not a
Pantomime, but a very graceful and poetical Fairy
Extravaganza. Rather dull, perhaps, but quite
refined, and containing nothing whatever that
could shock the sensibilities of the most fastidious.

(Foggerty's Fairy, Act I)

Foggerty's Fairy is one of W.S. Gilbert's funniest and most inventive plays, but also one of his least well known. Its central idea, that to make even the smallest alteration to the past leads to major changes in the present, may seem child's play to a modern audience brought up on the conventions of twentieth-century science fiction, but it was unfamiliar to many at the time. First performed at London's Criterion Theatre on the 15th of

December 1881, it bewildered critics and audiences alike. They generally agreed with the mixed assessment of *Reynolds' Paper*: 'It is a play full of original and witty conceit; but the plot is madness gone mad.' The *Referee* declared: '*Foggerty's Fairy* is a puzzle which wearies in the solution,' while the *Sportsman* judged the plot to be 'something too much like a proposition in the sixth book of Euclid to be followed by any average audience'. Despite its widely acknowledged wit and invention, it lasted for only twenty performances, closing on the 6th of January 1882.

However, the idea of the play originated much earlier. Gilbert had contributed an illustrated short story called 'The Story of a Twelfth Cake' to the Christmas number of the *Graphic* in 1874. It told the tale of confectioner Tommy Williamson, who is granted three wishes by a visiting fairy, enabling him to obliterate elements from his past – each wish flinging him into an ever-worse alternative present, until, with his final wish, he obliterates from his life the meeting with the fairy that had caused all the trouble in the first place.

Five years later, in 1879, having been commissioned by the actor Edward Askew Sothern to write a play, Gilbert recalled his old story and developed it into a wild farcical comedy. Sothern was best known in his time for creating the role of Lord Dundreary in Tom Taylor's comedy *Our American Cousin* (1858). Lord Dundreary, whose scenes were largely improvised by Sothern himself, was a comic character of genius, a brainless but whimsical aristocrat with a logic all his own:

Birds of *a* feather flock together: yes, that's it! As if a whole flock of birds would have only one feather! They'd all catch cold. Besides, there's only one of those birds could have that feather, and that fella would fly all on one side! That's one of those things no fella can find out. Besides, fancy any bird being such a d——d fool as to go into a corner and flock all by himself!

Lord Dundreary took the English-speaking world by storm. The extravagantly long side whiskers sported by Sothern's character became known as Dundrearies, and his eccentric sayings were known as Dundrearyisms. But the role became something of a millstone to Sothern, and he was always on the lookout for a part that could replace its success.

Sothern felt a great kinship with Gilbert's deadpan style of comedy, and regarded him as 'one of the shining lights of modern dramatic literature'. In fact, Sothern had commissioned a previous play from Gilbert, a comedy drama called *The Ne'er-Do-Weel*, which, after some discussion in 1876–77, he regretfully returned to Gilbert as being unsuited to his taste.

Nevertheless, Sothern retained great admiration for the dramatist, and eagerly embraced Gilbert's new play. *The Era*, the weekly paper of the theatrical profession, reported on the 29th of February 1880: 'Mr Sothern says that, although his new comedy, by Mr Gilbert, has cost him 3,000 guineas, he would not take 6,000 guineas for it now. It is a piece of the wildest absurdity ever perpetrated, and all the parts are immense.' The extravagant language is very typical of Sothern (his letters are full of block capitals and exclamation marks), but the enthusiasm was certainly genuine.

Tragically, however, Sothern's health was deteriorating rapidly. He wrote in a letter to the New York *Spirit of the Times* in July 1880: 'I have been, and still am, dangerously ill, and am under the charge of a celebrated physician in such nervous complaints, but so weak that I can scarcely crawl from room to room.' He was forced to cancel his engagements; the production of *Foggerty's Fairy* promised for October 1880 never happened. He died on the 21st of January 1881 at the age of 54.

After Sothern's death, the play was taken up by another leading light of theatrical comedy, the Criterion Theatre's actor-manager Charles Wyndham, who was well known for his production of farces, such as James Albery's scandalous *Pink Dominos* (1877). Uniting Wyndham and Gilbert's much-anticipated new farce must have seemed a sure recipe for success. Indeed, as *The Era* reported on 17 December, 'The audience assembled at the Criterion Theatre [for the first night] on Thursday evening was as friendly as it could possibly be.' However, as *The Referee* said, 'Criterion audiences assemble not to solve abstruse problems or to follow out the intricacies of a dramatic maze.' Frankly, the play's complexity baffled them.

The action begins on Frederick Foggerty's wedding day, when, just as he is on the verge of marrying Jenny Talbot, the proceedings are interrupted with the unexpected arrival on the scene of Delia Spiff, an old flame of Foggerty's. In extremis, Foggerty summons his guardian spirit, the Fairy Rebecca, and invokes a magic spell to eliminate Miss Spiff from his life. However, as Rebecca explains, 'if you obliterate an act and its consequences, it's impossible to say what incidents may or may not have taken their place. You are pretty nearly sure to find yourself in an entirely altered state of circumstances.' She also sets out an idea that is commonplace to us today, but which would have been much less so in 1881: the notion now called Butterfly Effect, which posits that the flapping of a butterfly's wings can lead to a tornado – or, indeed, that a chance encounter between two dogs can lead to the birth of a Lancashire Foggerty.

The events of Acts Two and Three hinge upon the audience's understanding of these notions, and on their ability to comprehend the difference between the world Foggerty thinks he is in and the world created by the elimination of Delia Spiff from his life. Anyone who has seen *Back to the Future* would have no trouble with *Foggerty's Fairy*; but unfortunately, no one in 1881 had seen *Back to the Future*.

A good number of the critics seemed to find the plot too much to comprehend. *The Stage* exclaimed: 'Never was an audience so completely at sea, and so thoroughly cast into wonderment and surprise as after the first act of *Foggerty's Fairy*,' while *The Daily Telegraph* grumbled: 'The dramatic scheme is as elaborate as a difficult equation in algebra, and the senses seem to swim under the influence of all this illogical logic and this apparently senseless sense.'

The critics generally praised the play's wit and inventiveness, but often with a weary sense that Gilbert had this time been rather *too* clever, as *The Era* opined:

It begins briskly, and all through there are comic ideas and quaint turns of expression such as no other dramatic author could have written. It is only fair to Mr Gilbert to say that, when these passages occurred, they were greeted with shouts of laughter. They were frequently so odd, so unexpected, as to take the audience by surprise. But the author's power to take his audience by storm is nothing new. Usually, however, he accomplishes this by novel sketches of character, and by completely reversing the ordinary conditions of human life. But in this comedy he has gone far beyond any previous attempt, for the entire piece is a surprise. In previous works Mr Gilbert's aim has been to set at nought everyday ideas, manners and customs; but in this wild piece of eccentricity he turns even stage traditions topsy-turvy…

The play had a mixed first-night reception. *The Era* noted 'occasional murmurs' from the audience, but also that Gilbert was called before the curtain at the end. As for the reviews, *The Sportsman* perhaps summarised the consensus best by calling the play 'more fog than fairy'.

To judge from pre-production scripts held by the British Library, it would appear that extensive revisions were made to it after the first night, especially to Act Three, during which the first-night audience had grown restive. But even this was not enough to save the play, and it closed after three weeks.

Its problem was, perhaps, a simple one of the wrong venue at the wrong time. *The Referee*'s statement that audiences at the Criterion did not attend the theatre in order to tax their brains was surely correct. Also, it was the Christmas season, the season of pantomime and broad slapstick, and the festive audiences were not in the mood for complex logical puzzles. It may be true, too, that the title *Foggerty's Fairy* gave audiences the wrong idea of what to expect.

And yet, at bottom, the play is a witty variation on Christmas entertainments. In it, a very theatrical fairy intervenes in mortal life to transform matters, much as the traditional pantomime fairy would do. The everyday mingles with the fantastic. Freddy Foggerty is at pains to be reassured that he will not be transformed into Harlequin, that staple of the harlequinade which traditionally concluded Victorian pantomimes – but in fact the whole play is really a sort of harlequinade. The script is full of volleys of unexpected wit which, as *The Era* acknowledged, the audience greeted with shouts of laughter, though the critic was sufficiently blasé about Gilbert's talent in this direction as to dismiss them as 'nothing new'.

Gilbert's obsession with the theatre went back almost as far as he could remember. In his 1868 article 'Getting Up a Pantomime' he frankly asserted that attending the pantomime was 'the only recollection of unmixed pleasure associated with early childhood':

Those night expeditions to a mystic building, where incomprehensible beings of all descriptions held astounding revels, under circumstances which I never endeavoured to account for, were, to my infant mind, absolute realisations of a fairy mythology which I had almost incorporated with my religious faith.

('Incomprehensible beings of all descriptions holding astounding revels' could almost be a manifesto for Gilbertian theatre, especially for Gilbert and Sullivan opera.)

Fairies recur throughout Gilbert's dramatic works, usually as agents of unintended havoc. It is perhaps significant that while, for instance, Shakespeare's fairies reach the mortal world via a forest glade, in Gilbert's works their gateway is generally to be found through some down-at-heel London theatre, where they might be discovered complaining about rheumatism or their position at the back of the chorus: because, to Gilbert, the theatre was a place of magic.

During the short run of *Foggerty's Fairy*, Gilbert was already occupied in writing another piece set in the world of the fairies: the Gilbert and Sullivan opera that would be called *Iolanthe*. He had written of fairies before, of course: seriously in *The Wicked World* (1873); satirically in *The Happy Land* the same year. *Foggerty's Fairy* reopened that imaginative seam, tempting him to flights of fancy that could barely be contained within the requirements of the play: a scene for the beginning of Act II, cut before opening night for clear practical reasons, shows the Fairy Rebecca at ease with her friends and discussing their weary lot (see Appendix). This little sketch, possibly written more for Gilbert's own amusement than with any real expectation of its reaching the stage, looks forward to the curiously 'human' fairies of *Iolanthe*. (It has been noted more than once that it is Sullivan's music that makes Gilbert's fairies fairylike; less often mentioned is the fact that it is Gilbert who makes them *believable*.)

After *Foggerty's Fairy* closed, Gilbert did not forget it. Ever thrifty, he reused some of its lines in *The Mikado*. He included the script in the third volume of his *Original Plays* in 1895, alongside some of his most successful works such as *The Mikado* and *The Gondoliers*. Perhaps most significantly, when in 1890 he published a collection of his short stories, he revised 'The Story of a Twelfth Cake', renaming it 'Foggerty's Fairy', and made it the title story of the whole collection. Despite the play's initial failure, it remained a work of which he was proud.

It has not had a fortunate afterlife, though it is sometimes produced by amateur societies in the UK and the US. Anthony Jenkins, the author of a study of Tom Stoppard's theatrical works, has championed *Foggerty's Fairy* (which, with its wit, cleverness and theatrical playfulness has, after all, much in common with Stoppard), calling it in his 1991 book *The Making of Victorian Drama* 'The one play of Gilbert's that ought to be revived.' It fizzes with wit and invention. It deserves to be better known.

ANDREW CROWTHER

FOGGERTY'S FAIRY

An entirely original fairy farce
in three acts

'On a banni les demons et les fees,
  Le raisonner tristement s'accredite:
On court, helas! apres la verite:
  Ah! croyer moi l'erreur a son merite!'

'Demons and fays are banished, hand in hand,
  Stern Common Sense has ousted Necromancy:
Though fact, alas, now lords it o'er the land:
  Trust me, there's something to be said for Fancy!'

VOLTAIRE[*]

DRAMATIS PERSONAE

FREDERICK FOGGERTY
WALKINSHAW } *young surgeons without practice*

TALBOT, *a wholesale cheesemonger*

DR LOBB
DR DOBB } *mad doctors*

BLOGG, *a mad keeper*

UNCLE FOGLE
WALKER
BALKER } *wedding guests*

THE FAIRY REBECCA

JENNIE TALBOT { *engaged in Act I to* FOGGERTY
engaged in Act II to WALKINSHAW

MISS DE VERE, *a romantic lady*

MISS DELIA SPIFF, *a matter-of-fact old lady*

LOTTIE
TOTTIE } JENNIE'*s bridesmaids*
AUNT BOGLE

ACT I

SCENE

Drawing room in TALBOT*'s house on the morning of his daughter's marriage to* FOGGERTY. *A large bow window leads into a garden.* TALBOT *is discovered. The following guests are disposed about the room:* UNCLE FOGLE *(a snuffy old gentleman),* AUNT BOGLE *(a stout lady),* WALKER *and* BALKER *(two young men) and others. All are in extremely low spirits, except* TALBOT, *who endeavours to infuse a little cheerfulness into the company. All wear favours.**

ALL *(sighing)*: Ah!

UNCLE FOGLE: Oh, dear me, dear me!

TALBOT: What *is* the matter with you all? Do try and be cheerful. If my only daughter *is* going to be married to a penniless young apothecary, there's no occasion to treat her wedding as though it were a funeral. Pray, pray remember that this is, after all, a festive occasion.

UNCLE FOGLE: My dear John, I wouldn't, for the world, say a word to cast a gloom over these – well, these rejoicings; but I can't help thinking that, with her attractions, Jenny might have looked a little higher. You understand, I don't *say* it – I confine myself to *thinking* it.

7

AUNT BOGLE: You see, John, you know so little of Mr Foggerty.

TALBOT: I knew him when he was a little boy of nine; he was a very clean little boy of nine.

BALKER: Ah! but a man's character is not formed at nine.

UNCLE FOGLE: However, it's no use crying over spilt milk.

AUNT BOGLE: Very true – what's done can't be helped.

WALKER: Except it's mutton – and then what's *underdone* can't be helped.

(*All smile sadly at* WALKER*'s joke.*)

TALBOT (*shaking* WALKER*'s hand*): Thank you, Tommy; it's very kind and thoughtful of you to make that joke.

WALKER: I'll make another presently.

TALBOT: Thank you. I'm sure you will. I won't forget it. God bless you, Tommy.

AUNT BOGLE: After all, Mr Foggerty *may* be a very respectable young man.

UNCLE FOGLE: Equally, of course, he may *not*; but let us not anticipate disaster.

TALBOT: What was I to do? Jenny has, somehow, got a ridiculous idea into her head that she could never love any man who had ever loved before, and she is weak enough to believe that she has found this monstrosity in Foggerty. I've told her all sorts of anecdotes to his disparagement – not exactly true ones, because I couldn't find out any – but the sort of anecdotes that I dare say are true if one only knew. It's a painful thing, gentleman, for a father to have to admit, but my undutiful girl won't believe me.

UNCLE FOGLE: It's a sad thing when a girl won't believe her own father!

WALKER: If she won't believe her own father, whose father will she believe?

(*All smile sadly at* WALKER*'s joke.*)

TALBOT: Thank you, my boy – thank you! It was just the same with poor, broken-hearted Walkinshaw. She fell in love with Walkinshaw because she thought *he* had never loved before, but she found out from Foggerty that Walkinshaw had already been engaged to somebody, so that settled *him*. Then she fell in love with Foggerty. We did all we could to fix him with an affair of some kind, but in vain; it's true we *did* rake up an old boyish flirtation of his, but he was rather young at the time – only nine – and it's not likely to have been serious.

AUNT BOGLE: I don't know – a boy who flirts at nine will flirt at ninety; that's *my* experience.

BALKER: Nine is a critical age – a man's character is often formed at nine.

TALBOT (*looking off*): But Jenny's coming down – she's in the highest possible spirits, and I don't want her to be depressed. Those who feel they really can't bear up had better, perhaps, go and shed some tears in the garden…

(*All go off except* AUNT BOGLE, UNCLE FOGLE *and* TALBOT.)

…and, those who remain, please remember that you've been asked in order to contribute to the general hilarity, and, for goodness' sake, don't forget that this is really and truly a festive occasion. Come, let us all smile.

(*All smile grimly as* JENNY *enters, in a flood of tears, and dressed in morning dress. She is followed by* LOTTIE *and* TOTTIE, *dressed as bridesmaids. She throws herself down on a chair, weeping bitterly.* LOTTIE *and* TOTTIE *comfort her.*)

JENNY (*weeping*): Oh dear! oh dear! What *shall* I do?

TALBOT: There's Jenny at it now! Bless my heart, she'll have a red nose at the church!

LOTTIE: There, there – don't cry – don't cry!

TOTTIE: It's sure to be all right – don't cry!

TALBOT: Now what is it, and why are you not dressed? What *are* you crying for?

JENNY: Oh, Papa, Papa – I'm to be married this morning, and—

TALBOT: She's to be married this morning, and she's crying about it! Isn't that like a woman? And whose fault is it, I should like to know?

JENNY: Oh, Papa, I'm not crying because – because I'm g-g-going to be married to Frederick – but I've g-got to be at the church in half an hour, and my dress hasn't come home yet. (*Fresh burst of grief.*) Oh dear! oh dear! What *shall* I do?

TALBOT: Dress not come home?

(*During all this* UNCLE FOGLE *and* AUNT BOGLE *preserve a ridiculous and immovable smile.*)

JENNY: No, it was tight under the arms, so I sent it back, and it was to have come home this evening, and I've nothing to wear!

AUNT BOGLE: Don't cry, child. I've my own wedding dress at home. It was made in 1820. I've never worn it but once. I'll lend it to you.

TALBOT: Why, that'll be the very thing.

JENNY (*sobbing*): No – no. You – you're too fat.

(UNCLE FOGLE *and* AUNT BOGLE, *who have been smiling fixedly all this time, suddenly look disgusted.*)

I mean, I'm too thin.

(*Exeunt* AUNT BOGLE *and* UNCLE FOGLE *in a huff.*)

Oh dear! What shall I do?

TALBOT: Come, come. I'll send for it. It'll be here directly. (*To* LOTTIE *and* TOTTIE:) Pick her up, my dears, pick her up, and, above all things, don't let her have a red nose at the church. Powder it, my dears; powder it. This is a festive occasion, and it absolutely must be powdered. (*Exit.*)

LOTTIE: There! It's sure to arrive in time.

TOTTIE: I'm sure I hope it will, if it's only to spite the ill-natured people who are always running Mr Foggerty down.

JENNY: I don't care what they say. He has one virtue that would sanctify him in my eyes though his errors were legion. He, at least, has never loved before.

LOTTIE: Well, it's possible, dear, of course.

JENNY: Possible! I have it on the very best authority. He told me so himself. *He* ought to know, I suppose.

TOTTIE: He *ought* to, dear, of course.

JENNY: Oh, would you have me doubt the man I love? Would you have me love the man I doubt? Oh no! no! Love doubts not. Doubt loves not. He says he has never loved, and it is enough.

LOTTIE (*to* TOTTIE): I'm sure I hope he hasn't, for if she found out too late that he had deceived her, what would she do?

(*Exeunt* LOTTIE *and* TOTTIE.)

JENNY (*dreamingly*): What would I do? I don't know. It would be something with a knife in it, and there would be blood. I don't know whose – perhaps his – perhaps mine! Oh, I dare not think of it! I dare not think of it!

(*Enter* FOGGERTY, *sticking a flower in his buttonhole.*)

FOGGERTY: There. It's wonderful how a tastily selected vegetable sets one off. (*Sees* JENNY.) Jenny! My own! Why, not dressed yet? What's the matter?

JENNY (*dreamily*): I say I dare not think of it.

FOGGERTY: Why not?

JENNY (*dreamily*): There would be blood, wouldn't there?

FOGGERTY: If you dressed yourself? No, I don't see why there should. There, go and put on your things.

JENNY (*dreamily*): Yours or mine?

FOGGERTY: Yours, of course. What do you mean?

JENNY: I mean, if I found out that you had ever loved
another—

FOGGERTY: Oh, of course, in that case mine; I would shed
it myself.

JENNY: But you never have?

FOGGERTY: I? Never!

JENNY: This flirtation – when you were nine?

FOGGERTY: It was nothing. She made eyes at me in
church.

JENNY: And what did you do?

FOGGERTY: I fled.

JENNY: In horror?

FOGGERTY: In horror. It was so bold of her. I was appalled.

JENNY: My delicate-minded Frederick! Oh, he has never
loved till now!

FOGGERTY: Jenny, we are to be married today; do you
think I might—

JENNY: I think so, dear; it is our wedding day.

FOGGERTY: Under the circumstances, I think. (*Kisses her.
Both sigh.*)

JENNY: I don't know how it is, it's very strange and unaccountable and unwomanly; but, although my dress
don't fit, I feel almost happy!

FOGGERTY: I am glad you are happy, Jenny.

JENNY: I have always said that my love should only be
given to one who had never loved before. I will not
have a heart at second-hand. *My* husband must be
one whose torch of love was lit by me alone, and you
are such an one, are you not?

FOGGERTY: Yes; many a night and oft have I lain awake
gazing at the moon, and wondering what manner

of thing this love might be of which I had heard so much, this strange and irrational desire to spend a lifetime with the adored object; and, when I renewed my old acquaintance with you, the sun broke on my darkness, and all seemed clear as summer noon!

JENNY: My darling!

FOGGERTY: *Do* you think I might again?

JENNY: Yes, dear, I think so.

FOGGERTY: No, no – better not – better not.

JENNY: In *my* eyes, a man who has once loved is as a defaced postage stamp – interesting, perhaps, to the collector, but to all others a thing of naught.

FOGGERTY: Such as poor Walkinshaw, for example.

JENNY: Such as poor Mr Walkinshaw. I do not think I ever loved him, but he interested me because I believed that I was the first that had ever kindled the fire of love within his heart. But, to my horror and disgust, before we had been engaged a fortnight I learnt from you that he had already loved another.

FOGGERTY: I felt it to be my duty not to conceal from you a fact so material to your happiness, my poor child.

JENNY: Poor then, but poor no longer. Rich in the devotion of a heart that throbs for me, and me alone!

FOGGERTY: Oh! don't you think I might venture once more, to… No, no. We can wait – we can wait.

(*Enter* WALKINSHAW. *He is in a most depressed condition, but gorgeously dressed, nevertheless.*)

JENNY: Mr Walkinshaw!

WALKINSHAW: Nay, don't mind me. Proceed with your fondlings. Time was when I could not have witnessed them. But I must get used to it – it's good practice. Go on.

JENNY: It's your own fault, Mr Walkinshaw. You led me to believe that yours was a virgin heart.

FOGGERTY: Too bad, Walkinshaw – too bad.

WALKINSHAW (*furiously*): Foggerty, I submit to Miss Talbot's reproaches, for I respect and sympathise with the feelings that give them birth. But from you I will *not* stand it. Take care, sir – take care!

JENNY: Wouldn't you rather retire, Mr Walkinshaw? It *must* pain you to see us like this.

WALKINSHAW: No – I must learn to bear it. Go on; but do it by degrees. Put your arm around her waist, Foggerty. There – let me get used to that first. (*Writhes in anguish.*)

JENNY: If you had been all that you represented yourself to be, you would today have stood in Frederick's place, and he would, very likely, have been *your* best man.

WALKINSHAW: And bad would have been the best! Miss Talbot, it is true that I had already loved, but whom? A woman who lived on actions for breach of promise* – who had already brought eighteen such actions, and who was seeking every opportunity to make me the defendant in a nineteenth. Foggerty, oblige me by allowing Miss Talbot to rest her head on your shoulder.

FOGGERTY: Do you mean it?

(*She does so.*)

WALKINSHAW: Oh, it is hard to bear! It is hard to bear! (*Writing.*) Now kiss her.

(FOGGERTY *does so.*)

Oh!!! (*Writhing.*)

JENNY: Mr Walkinshaw, you deliberately deceived me, and I can never believe you again.

FOGGERTY: I'm surprised at you, Walkinshaw, I am indeed.

WALKINSHAW: Miss Talbot, I admit that I deceived you. Still, if you will so far forget the past as to extend credence to me when I tell you, on the faith and honour of a broken-hearted gentleman, that your wedding dress has just arrived, you will pour one drop of balm into a wound that has hitherto yawned balmless.

JENNY: My wedding dress arrived! And *you* brought it! Oh, thank you, thank you. Mr Walkinshaw, there is much that is very nice about you. Oh, why did you deceive me once? But for that I might even now be… But no (*looking at* FOGGERTY), it is better as it is! (*Exit.*)

FOGGERTY: Ha! ha! ha! poor Walkinshaw!

WALKINSHAW: Cheat! impostor! snake!

FOGGERTY: Not at all, Walkinshaw. I've merely profited by your example.

WALKINSHAW: Oh, this is hard – this is bitterly hard! However, you're not married yet; that's one comfort.

FOGGERTY: No; but I shall be in half an hour – and that's another.

WALKINSHAW: Don't be too sure; I have news for you. Delia Spiff, your late fiancée, arrived from Melbourne yesterday.

FOGGERTY: Are you in earnest?

WALKINSHAW: Look at that. (*Hands newspaper.*)

FOGGERTY (*reads*): Blackball Line – *Red Knight* – specie – passengers on board – Miss Delia Spiff! What's to be done? She'll come here of course! The Talbots are her only living relatives! Why, she may arrive at any moment, and if she should—

WALKINSHAW (*sternly*): It would be a just retribution. You trifled with her, sir!

FOGGERTY: Trifled with her? Nonsense! You *can't* trifle with an old woman with a green umbrella. Besides, I was in Melbourne, starving, penniless. There, under my very nose, so to speak, was a comic old dowager, absolutely rolling in banknotes and sound securities – rolling in them, sir – under my very nose! What was I to do?

WALKINSHAW: A man of proper feeling would have looked the other way.

FOGGERTY: I had the banknotes before my eyes; they dazzled me. I didn't see the dowager – at least not clearly – until some weeks after I proposed to her. As soon as my eyes got used to the glare of the money the dowager dawned upon me.

WALKINSHAW: How did she look?

FOGGERTY: Fearful! I couldn't do it. I couldn't, indeed. *You* couldn't do it. I didn't like to tell her so, so I implied it gently and delicately. In fact, I bolted, and came to England. I found Jenny, the friend of my childhood, young and cheerful. She was engaged to you; but, nevertheless, she was quite cheerful. I felt it to be my duty to let her know how basely you had deceived her. You were dismissed, and I stepped into your shoes, in the assumed character of a gentleman who had never loved before. And in half an hour I marry her.

WALKINSHAW: Supposing, always, that Spiff don't turn up.

FOGGERTY: Walkinshaw, she *shan't* turn up. I won't give her time to turn up; we'll be off at once. (*Impatiently:*) What are we waiting for? Why don't they come? Why don't we start? What an extraordinary thing it is that a woman cannot be punctual! (*Calling:*) Jenny, are you ready? What! 'Five minutes?' It's an unreasonable time. Can't you come as you are? 'Impossible?' Ridiculous! (*Getting more impatient:*) What *is* the reason of this preposterous delay? Why does everything go wrong today? (*Pulling* WALKINSHAW *about:*) Why have you got a confounded green waistcoat, and a ridiculous red tie?

WALKINSHAW: Don't! I'm dressed for a wedding!

FOGGERTY: Dressed for a wedding? You're dressed for a lobster salad! (*To footstool:*) You get out! (*Kicking it:*) You're always in the way!

WALKINSHAW (*at door*): This is what it is to play with women's hearts! But a terrible revenge will be mine. The wedding breakfast has yet to be eaten, and I supply the wine. (*Exit.*)

FOGGERTY: Upon my soul, I believe I'm the unluckiest dog breathing! I did think I was safe this time. She'll come here, of course – and then... Why don't that girl come? (*Calling:*) Jenny, do come along! Never mind the hooks and eyes. You can do them in the carriage. What? 'Couldn't think of such a thing'? There, isn't that a woman all over? Dress – dress – dress. Always dressing, and never done with it. (*Looking at watch:*) Half-past eleven! We shan't get to the church for an hour – and if Delia *should* turn up! It's fearful – it's more than fearful. It's appalling! It's a fix that nothing short of a fairy godmother could get me out of. Why haven't I a fairy godmother? People used to have them. You had only to invite them to your christening, and they'd do anything for you. Now, I call that gratitude. But fairy godmothers are out of fashion now, and gratitude went out with them. Still, if there is such a thing as a guardian angel watching over me, here is an opportunity to show what she's worth that may never occur again.

(*Slow music. The wall opens, and the fairy* REBECCA *is discovered standing in front of a revolving star. He does not see her, but he hears the slow music.*)

There's a confounded German band outside, with the clarionet* out of tune, as usual.

REBECCA (*coming down*): Mr Foggerty!

FOGGERTY: Eh! (*Turns and sees her.*) Hallo! I beg your pardon, but—

REBECCA: You don't know me?

FOGGERTY: I – that is… Well, no, I *don't* know you.

REBECCA: I'm the Fairy Rebecca!

FOGGERTY: The Fairy Rebecca?

REBECCA: Yes; don't be frightened. I'm a good fairy.

FOGGERTY: Now, you be off; we've nothing for you. Come, away you go.

REBECCA: You don't believe me?

FOGGERTY: No, I don't believe you.

REBECCA (*humbly*): Upon my word, I'm speaking the truth. I really am a fairy, I am indeed. Didn't you see me appear?

FOGGERTY: No.

REBECCA: I came through that wall – right through it!

FOGGERTY: Can you disappear through it?

REBECCA: Certainly.

FOGGERTY: Then the sooner you do it the better.

REBECCA (*going towards wall*): I think you're extremely unkind. I came simply because I thought I might be of use to you. But if you don't want me…

FOGGERTY: Stop. Are you, by any chance, in earnest?

REBECCA: Of course I'm in earnest; but it's the old story. Nobody believes in us nowadays. Time was when we mixed ourselves up, as a matter of course, in human business. We were a power then, and people were afraid of us. Whenever an important christening took place we were invited as a matter of course, and if any one of us was neglected, it was bad for the baby. Ah, those *were* days!

FOGGERTY: But that was some time ago. We don't associate ladies of your calling with frock coats and trousers.

REBECCA: Exactly; and so our existence is reduced to a mere question of tailoring. If tights and trunks came in again, I suppose we should come in again with them.

FOGGERTY: I trust not. I *trust* not.

REBECCA: Why not?

FOGGERTY: Because they are not usually worn by ladies.

REBECCA (*pettishly*): *Come into fashion* with them! One has to pick one's words in speaking to you – you are so matter of fact.

FOGGERTY: It's a matter-of-fact age.

REBECCA: Not particularly. Every age is matter of fact to those who live in it. Romance died the day before yesterday. Today will be romantic the day after tomorrow.

FOGGERTY: Yes. Perhaps if you looked in again the day after tomorrow—

REBECCA: I'm speaking metaphorically. Don't be ridiculous. Now then, business. I'm your tutelary* fairy.

FOGGERTY: My what?

REBECCA: Your tutelary fairy – your guardian genius. I hover over you – like this. (*Hovers.*) You know what I mean.

FOGGERTY: Am I to understand that you're always hovering over me when I don't know it?

REBECCA: Certainly.

FOGGERTY: Oh!

REBECCA: What's the matter?

FOGGERTY: Nothing. It's embarrassing, that's all. I wish I'd known it before! Has this hovering been going on long?

REBECCA: About eighteen months – ever since your engagement to Delia Spiff. The fact is I was sorry to see a fine young man throwing himself away on a ridiculous old woman, so I said to myself, 'That

young man's making a fool of himself; I'll keep my
eye on that young man.'

FOGGERTY: Oh! you know about Delia Spiff?

REBECCA: To be sure. We *all* know about it. It's a standing joke up in Fairyland.

FOGGERTY: Is it? It's rather a serious matter down here.
But – can I offer you anything?

REBECCA: Thank you. I'll take a glass of sherry and a
biscuit. (*He helps her. She drinks.*) Now, then, what's
the difficulty?

FOGGERTY: Oh, it's about that woman; she's the bane
of my life! I'm on the point of being married to a
most delightful girl, and I'm expecting Spiff to turn
up every moment and claim me.

REBECCA: Ah! I thought as much! Well, what do you
want me to do? I can't strangle Delia, you know,
because I'm a good fairy.

FOGGERTY: What a pity.

REBECCA (*with alacrity*): Yes; but I know a bad fairy
who'd do it at once if I asked her.

FOGGERTY: No, no! I don't want to hurt Delia; but if
you *could* manage to marry her offhand to somebody – to Walkinshaw, for instance—

REBECCA: No, it would be too hard on Walkinshaw. You
see I'm a good fairy! The bad fairy I was speaking
about would do it with pleasure if I asked her; but
it would take time, and I suppose time is precious.

FOGGERTY (*looking at his watch*): It is indeed. It's very
annoying, for that woman's been the curse of my
existence. All my misfortunes have had their origin in my engagement to her, and if I could blot

her out of my existence I should be the happiest man alive.

REBECCA (*musing*): Blot her out of your existence? Well, I think I could do that for you.

FOGGERTY (*delighted*): You could!

REBECCA (*considering*): Ye-es, there's no difficulty at all about that; but—

FOGGERTY: Then I'll do it!

REBECCA: Don't be in a hurry. Think what you're about. If you blot Delia Spiff out of your career, you blot out at the same time all the consequences that came of having known her.

FOGGERTY: But, my good girl, that's exactly what I want to do!

REBECCA: Take care. The consequences of an act are often much more numerous and important than people have any idea of. Take your own case: you come of a good family, and you are proud of it.

FOGGERTY: We are the Lancashire Foggertys.

REBECCA: No doubt. *You* didn't do much towards it, and I don't see what you've got to be proud of; but still, proud you are. Now, you would never have been born if your father had never met your mother.

FOGGERTY: I suppose not.

REBECCA: And your father met your mother in this wise: some thirty-six years ago, as he was walking down Regent Street, his attentions were directed to a sculptor's shop, in which was a remarkable monument to a Colonel Culpepper, who died of a cold caught in going into the Ganges to rescue a favourite dog which had fallen into it. An old schoolfellow passed by, and, touching your father on the shoulder, asked him to dinner. Your father went, and at the dinner met your mother, whom he eventually married. And that's how *you* came about.

FOGGERTY: I see. If my father hadn't had that invitation to dinner I should never have been born.

REBECCA: No doubt; but your existence is primarily due to a much more remote cause. If your father hadn't loitered opposite the sculptor's shop, his schoolfellow would never have met him. If Colonel Culpepper hadn't died, your father would never have stopped to look at his monument. If Colonel Culpepper's favourite dog had never tumbled into the Ganges, the Colonel would never have caught the cold that led to his death. If that favourite dog's father had never met that favourite dog's mother that favourite dog would never have been born – neither would *you*. And yet you're proud of your origin!

FOGGERTY: I see. I never looked at it in that light. It's humiliating for a Lancashire Foggerty.

REBECCA: It *is* humiliating. Well, now you see where you are, and you can do as you like. Here is a small phial and a box of prepared pills. When you wish to eliminate a factor from your social equation, all you have to do is express your wish and swallow the draught. When you wish to see me, all you have to do is express your wish and swallow a pill. But take my advice: don't use it except in the last extremity. Remember, if you obliterate an act and its consequences, it's impossible to say what incidents may or may not have taken their place. You are pretty nearly sure to find yourself in an entirely altered state of circumstances.

FOGGERTY: I understand. But—

REBECCA: Yes?

FOGGERTY: There's one question I should like to ask – this is not a pantomime?

REBECCA: Bless the man, no.

FOGGERTY: It won't end in my being changed into Harlequin, and Jenny into Columbine, or any nonsense of that sort, will it? Because if it does—

REBECCA: You need not alarm yourself. This is not a Pantomime, but a very graceful and poetical Fairy Extravaganza. Rather dull, perhaps, but quite refined, and containing nothing whatever that could shock the sensibilities of the most fastidious.

FOGGERTY: That's quite sufficient. You understand the nature of my objection?

REBECCA: Perfectly—

FOGGERTY: It wouldn't be dignified—

REBECCA: I quite understand.

FOGGERTY: A Lancashire Foggerty jumping through a window!*

REBECCA: Oh! it wouldn't do at all. Well, I must be off now, for I've got to dance second in a ballet in a fairy glen in half an hour. Remember, when you eliminate an act from your career, all its consequences, direct and indirect, are eliminated with it; so take my advice, and don't use it except in a last emergency. (*Looking around:*) Where's my vampire?* Oh! I see – thank you. (*Placing herself opposite vampire.*) All right. Go!

(*Vampire opens. She steps into it, it closes, and she disappears. Hurried music.*)

FOGGERTY (*bewildered*): So I've a guardian spirit, have I? I'm a sort of human ward in fairy chancery,* and wherever I go, and whatever I do, there's a supernatural lady always at hand, popping in upon me when I least expect it, and looking down upon me when I haven't an idea of it. It's complimentary – it's even gratifying – but it's distinctly embarrassing. I'll defy any man to feel unconstrained and at his ease when he knows that there's an invisible young woman at his elbow all day long; and as for this phial – how do I know that my position will be improved if I use it? I don't like these unknown incidents that she alludes to. There's such a thing a getting out of the frying pan into the fire. By Jove, when I think of the difficulties and dangers with which I'm surrounded, I feel uncommonly inclined to begin at the beginning, and wish that Colonel Culpepper's favourite dog's father had remained a bachelor to the end of his days!

(*Enter* JENNY *in wedding dress, followed by* LOTTIE *and* TOTTIE.)

Oh, here you are at last. Now let's be off.
JENNY: And haven't you a word to say about my dress?
FOGGERTY: Eh, what? Oh, beautiful, beautiful. Now, do come!
LOTTIE: Isn't it lovely! Isn't it quite too charming?

TOTTIE: And look at the lace! It's Venetian point. And the bouquet! and do look at the wreath! It's absolutely heavenly.

FOGGERTY: Damn the wreath!

JENNY: Oh! (*Bursts into tears.*) Oh dear! did you hear what he said?

(*Enter* OLD TALBOT *and* WALKINSHAW, *with the other guests from garden.*)

FOGGERTY: Here you are at last!

TALBOT: Yes, all ready. Now then. (*Sees* JENNY *crying.*) Why, what's the matter now? You've got your dress, and what more do you want?

JENNY (*crying*): Oh, Papa! It's Frederick!

TALBOT: What has he done? Don't he like the dress?

JENNY: Yes – yes, he – he likes the dress, but – but – he damned the wreath!

TALBOT (*horrified*): Foggerty, did you seriously damn that wreath?

FOGGERTY: Well, I damned it, but not seriously. It was a figure of speech.

TALBOT (*to* JENNY, *who is whimpering*): There, there, you hear. It was a figure of speech. (*To the others:*) It was a poetical metaphor. A man may be allowed to indulge in a poetical metaphor on his wedding day.

WALKER: If a man may not be allowed to indulge in a poetical metaphor on his own wedding day, on whose wedding day *may* he?

ALL (*sighing*): Ah!

UNCLE FOGLE: I cannot refrain, even at this supreme moment, from—

FOGGERTY: Stop – I know what you're going to say. I'm utterly unworthy of her. With her money, she might have done much better, and, no doubt, there's a good deal against me, if you only knew it. *That's* what you were going to say. Isn't it?

ALL: It is.

UNCLE FOGLE: That sort of thing.

FOGGERTY: Well, then, I quite agree with you. It's carried unanimously. Now, let the subject drop.

TALBOT: Jenny, take my arm; Uncle Fogle, offer your arm to Aunt Bogle; Walker, take Lottie; Balker, take Tottie; Foggerty, you follow with Walkinshaw, as a matter of course. (*To all, who are looking very miserable:*) Now, my dear friends, can't you manage to get up a smile? This is not a funeral.

AUNT BOGLE: Very true. Let us all smile.

(*All smile except* WALKINSHAW, *who is scowling.*)

TALBOT: Walkinshaw, if you don't smile you shall go home.

JENNY: Oh, Mr Walkinshaw, pray smile, for my sake!

WALKINSHAW: For *your* sake? (*Sighs; then, with an effort:*) For your sake I will! (*Assumes a forced smile.*)

TALBOT: That's it – capital! and whatever you do, mind you keep that up. Now, then, away we go!

(*They move towards door, when it opens, and* MISS DELIA SPIFF *enters. She is a very eccentric-looking old lady, and carries a large green umbrella.*)

MISS SPIFF: Stop!

ALL: Who is this?

FOGGERTY (*horrified*): Delia Spiff! I knew it! I'm a ruined man!

JENNY: Why, I declare it's Aunt Delia!

ALL: Aunt Delia?

MISS SPIFF: Yes; Aunt Spiff, arrived at Victoria Docks this morning, from Melbourne.

JENNY: Why, how fortunate! You're just in time for my wedding!

MISS SPIFF: Your wedding? Whom are you going to marry?

TALBOT: Mr Frederick Foggerty.

MISS SPIFF: Oh, indeed!

FOGGERTY (*confused*): Delighted, I'm sure.

MISS SPIFF (*to* FOGGERTY): Well, you're a pretty fellow, *you* are!

JENNY: Frederick is generally admired.

MISS SPIFF (*to* FOGGERTY): So I've caught you at last, have I?

JENNY: What do you mean?

MISS SPIFF: That young man belongs to *me*!

ALL: What!

MISS SPIFF: Here it is – black and white. (*Producing document:*) He admired me. I can't imagine what he saw in me to admire, but he saw something. I attracted him; he grew attentive. I fascinated him; he grew sentimental. I was coy; he proposed to me. I accepted him; he grew indifferent. I sang to him; he wearied of me. I danced before him; he fled!

WALKINSHAW: Oh, Foggerty, for shame! Too bad.

TALBOT (*dismally*): You needn't smile any more at present, gentlemen.

JENNY: Frederick, what does this mean?

FOGGERTY: I believe she refers to me. It's nothing. It's a figure of speech, a mere form, commonly employed by elderly Australian ladies in – in renewing a – a Platonic acquaintance. (*Relapses.*)

TALBOT: You hear? It's a figure of speech, a flight of metaphor – nothing more.

WALKER: If an elderly Australian lady may not be allowed to indulge in a flight of metaphor on renewing a Platonic acquaintance, who may?

TALBOT: To be sure. Thank you, Walker. (*To company:*) It's all right, you can smile again.

(*All smile mechanically.*)

MISS SPIFF: Stuff and nonsense. There ain't much metaphor about *me*. I'm a plain fact.

FOGGERTY: A hideous fact!

JENNY (*with an effort*): Aunt Delia, am I to understand that Mr Frederick Foggerty offered marriage to you?

MISS SPIFF (*indignantly*): Why, to be sure you are! What do you suppose he offered?

JENNY: It is well. I renounce him. You can go home, everybody. There will be no wedding today. Oh, Papa, Papa! to think that even *he* has loved before! (*Sobs on* TALBOT*'s breast.*)

TALBOT (*to company, who have preserved their fixed smile through this*): You needn't smile now, gentlemen.

(*All scowl.*)

FOGGERTY: Jenny – I haven't – I didn't – it – it was a Platonic engagement.

MISS SPIFF: A Platonic fiddlestick!

FOGGERTY: Miss Spiff, you will not insist on your bond. You will be merciful! You will not dash the cup – dash it, the *jug* of happiness from my lips. You have a great heart, and so you will not do these things!

MISS SPIFF: Won't I? Come to the altar! (*Collaring him.*)*

TALBOT: But my good woman—

MISS SPIFF: Woman yourself. (*To* FOGGERTY*:*) Come to joy!

TALBOT: Now, pray do be reasonable. Pray do let's have a little common sense.

MISS SPIFF: You shall. You want it. Hark ye, sir. You are in trade?

TALBOT: I am. Wholesale.

MISS SPIFF: So am I. Wholesale. What's *your* stock?

TALBOT: Mine's cheese.

MISS SPIFF: Mine's charms. It's a small business. There ain't many of them, and what there are ain't much to speak of. The stock's damaged, isn't it?

TALBOT: Well, as for that, I can hardly be so ungallant as to admit to a lady's face, that – that—

MISS SPIFF: Stuff and nonsense. Is it damaged or is it not? Come! Out with it. Yes, or no?

TALBOT: Well, if you put it in that way, it *is* damaged.

MISS SPIFF: Not the sort of goods that one can get off one's hands every day of the week?

TALBOT: Oh, I don't say that. I can quite understand, for instance, that a snug, elderly gentleman, with a comfortable independence, would—

MISS SPIFF (*abruptly*): Will *you* have me?

TALBOT (*taken aback*): God bless me, no!

MISS SPIFF: Of course you wouldn't, and you're right. *I* wouldn't if I was you. Well, I've had a bid from that ridiculous young man. I knocked myself down to him and he fled.

FOGGERTY (*on the sofa, feebly*): In all cases of dispute the goods to be put up again and knocked down to the highest bidder.

MISS SPIFF: But there ain't any dispute. Here it is – black and white. (*Producing document.*) 'I, Frederick Foggerty, agree to marry you, Delia Spiff,' and so on. I had it stamped. Business.

FOGGERTY: Jenny, once more, save me from this catastrophe! After all, you are rich, and it's a mere question of compensation!

JENNY: Away, sir! I regard you with horror! You have deceived a trusting young heart!

MISS SPIFF: And a suspicious old one!

AUNT BOGLE: Go, viper! We expected something of this sort.

TALBOT: But—

MISS SPIFF (*collaring* FOGGERTY): Come to the altar – come to joy.

TALBOT: This is most exasperating – on a festive occasion! Confound you, why didn't you turn up before, ma'am? That wedding dress wasn't made under twenty pounds, and it's wasted! Then there's

the breakfast, and the carriages, and a new pair of
trousers bought expressly for the occasion!

MISS SPIFF: Don't distress yourself. I'll take them off your
hands.

TALBOT: They're not on my hands – they're on my legs,
and I won't have them taken off on any account!

MISS SPIFF (*to* FOGGERTY): Now, sir, are you ready?

FOGGERTY: Talbot, won't you say a word for me? Uncle
Fogle, Aunt Bogle, Lottie, Tottie, Walker, Balker?

(*All turn from him.*)

UNCLE FOGLE: Not a word, sir. We felt sure of this all
along, but, from motives of delicacy, we didn't *say* so.
We confined ourselves to *thinking* it.

LOTTIE: We consider that Jenny had had a most fortunate
escape.

TOTTIE: And we hope it will be a lesson to you for the
future.

FOGGERTY: It's all over. I'm lost!* Lead me away!

MISS SPIFF: Come to joy!

FOGGERTY: Stop! The draught! Rebecca's draught! I
forgot that! Matters couldn't look worse than they
are. It's a desperate remedy, but it's my only way out
of it! (*Staggers.*) Oh! oh! Help! I'm fainting!

JENNY: Gracious, he's fainting.

(*They wheel the sofa.* JENNY *rushes to him and supports him; he
struggles to loosen his collar.*)

MISS SPIFF: Fainting? Here's a pin. Prick him.

JENNY (*to* MISS SPIFF): You brute! The eau de cologne – quick!

FOGGERTY (*gasping, and kicking violently, on the sofa*): My tie, undo it! My waistcoat! Give me air! Give me water! Quick! quick! Water – water – water!

JENNY (*in great distress*): Oh, give him water – give him water, somebody!

(WALKINSHAW *has poured out a glass of water and handed it to him. Slow music to end of act.*)

FOGGERTY (*rising and deliberately pouring the contents of the phial into the glass of water*): Ladies and gentlemen, I deliberately wish that my acquaintance with Miss Spiff, and all its consequences, may henceforward be blotted out of my existence!

(*They all fall back in astonishment as* FOGGERTY *drinks. He falls insensible on the sofa. All group round him as he falls.*)

PICTURE

ACT II

SCENE

*A handsomely furnished back drawing room in Harley Street.
A wedding bouquet on table.* FOGGERTY *is discovered asleep on
a sofa. Enter* FAIRY REBECCA *through trap in stage.**

REBECCA (*looking at* FOGGERTY): Well, it's about time to
wake him. Poor fellow, he little thinks how materi-
ally his acquaintance with Miss Spiff has affected his
subsequent adventures! Now that he has obliterated
her and all the complicated consequences that came
of his having known her, he won't know whether he's
on his head or his heels. I'm really rather sorry for
him. However, I mustn't allow sentiment to interfere
with duty. It's time to wake him, so here goes.

(*Waves wand.* FOGGERTY *yawns, stretches himself and wakes.*)

FOGGERTY (*half awake*): Hallo! I've been asleep. (*Yawns.*)
Dreaming too! What queer things dreams are!
I dreamt that a fairy appeared to me and gave me an
ounce bottle, and told me that if I swallowed the contents— (*Sees the phial in his hand.*) Hallo! steady man,
steady – pull yourself together! Why, as I am alive, here
it is. The very one. (*Reads direction label.*) 'To obliterate a

circumstance, take two teaspoonfuls in a glass of water.'
Then it couldn't have been a dream! I remember it all
now. I was on the point of being married to Jenny – and
Spiff turned up – and I determined to blot out Spiff –
and I suppose I *have* blotted her out. (*Looking round:*) At
all events, she isn't here. (*Sees* REBECCA.) Hallo!

REBECCA: Hallo!

FOGGERTY: Well! here we are again!*

REBECCA: Yes, here we are again.

FOGGERTY: So Spiff's blotted out?

REBECCA: Yes, Spiff's done with; no more Spiff.

FOGGERTY: No chance of her coming back, eh?

REBECCA: None whatever. Your acquaintance with Spiff
and all its consequences are blotted out of your
existence.

FOGGERTY: Come, that's something. But I don't know
this room. Where am I?

REBECCA: You're where you would have been if you'd
never known Spiff.

FOGGERTY: Of course I am; but where's that?

REBECCA: Can't tell, I'm sure.

FOGGERTY: Don't you know?

REBECCA: I don't say I don't know; I only say I can't tell.

FOGGERTY: Doesn't it occur to you that for a guardian
spirit you take a rather airy and, if I may so express
myself, philosophical view of your duties?

REBECCA: A guardian spirit? Oh, I'm not your guardian
spirit now.

FOGGERTY: The deuce you're not?

REBECCA: Oh dear, no; that's all over – wiped out with
Spiff.

FOGGERTY: And *why* wiped out with Spiff?

REBECCA: You will recollect that I became your guardian spirit because I was sorry to see a fine young man throw himself away upon such an old scarecrow as Spiff.

FOGGERTY: Well?

REBECCA: But as you haven't thrown yourself away upon Spiff, the occasion for my services hasn't arisen. You see, you never knew Spiff.

FOGGERTY: Oh. May I ask if any other friends have been Spiffed out?

REBECCA: Once more, I'm not at liberty to say. (*Going to trap:*) You'll excuse me, I'm sure.

FOGGERTY: But you're not going without giving me some clue to my position?

REBECCA: I must; I can't help you. You must find it all out for yourself. I'm due at a Transformation Scene to change a respectable young plumber and a good plain cook into Harlequin and Columbine, and the gas is a serious item. I'm sorry I can't be of any further service to you; but, you see, I'm Spiffed out! Good morning. (*On trap:*) Go! (*She stamps her foot and disappears through trap.*)

FOGGERTY (*in bewilderment*): But, here, I say! I've no idea where I am, or who I am, or how I'm here, or whose house this is, and how I came into it – or, for that matter, whose trousers these are, and how I came into *them*! What am I to do? I can't go about asking people if they'll kindly tell me who I am, or if they'll be so obliging as to inform me where I live, or what I did yesterday, or what I've arranged to do tomorrow; they'd take me for a lunatic! And Jenny, how about Jenny? Is *she* Spiffed out? No, no. I knew her long before I knew Spiff. So that can't be. Now, let me see. I was on the point of being married to Jenny when Spiff turned up and prevented the marriage. But Spiff's obliterated. So, of course the marriage went on, and of course I'm married to Jenny. By the by, I wonder if I've been married to her long? I hope not. When you're head over ears in love with a girl, as I was with Jenny, it's disappointing to go to sleep and wake up and find that you've been married to her ever so long, and got tired of her, as I'll be bound I have of Jenny. (*Finds a letter in his pocket.*) Hallo! Here's a letter. It's addressed to me – and opened! Now, who the deuce has dared to open letters addressed to me? Oh! I suppose *I* did. I don't recollect doing it, but that doesn't seem to signify. (*Reads:*) 'Dearest, take heart.' Hallo! this is not Jenny's hand! (*Resumes.*) 'Dearest, take heart. Situated as we are towards one another, I do not think it would be quite prudent in me to call upon you.' No, I should think not! 'Nevertheless, in the course of tomorrow, I hope to be in a position to remove, for ever, the crushing load of anxiety under which you have so long laboured.' That's all! No signature. Humph! It seems that I'm infernally anxious about something; it would be convenient to know what it is. I'll ask Jenny. But stop a moment – perhaps Jenny doesn't know of this letter. Now, I wonder if she knows of it. I'll be bound she *doesn't* know of it. There's something about this letter – I don't know what – but something – that suggests that in all probability I shouldn't have shown it to her. Humph! I am extremely sorry to say that, notwith-standing the strictness of my principles, circumstances seem to point to the fact that I've been going it.

(*Enter* LOTTIE *and* TOTTIE *in the bonnets and dresses they wore in Act* I.)

LOTTIE: Oh, Mr Foggerty!

FOGGERTY: Lottie! Tottie! I'm delighted to see you. I'm delighted to find that *you're* not Spiffed out.

TOTTIE: Not Spiffed out? Oh, but we flatter ourselves that we *are* spiffed out;* at all events, we've got our best dresses on.

LOTTIE: I should think so; on this day of all others.

FOGGERTY: Of course; but I didn't mean that. Never mind. (*Aside:*) Now, by a judicious course of pumping, I shall find out exactly how I'm situated. (*Aloud:*) Well, what is it?

TOTTIE (*giving card*): A lady has sent this up, and says she must see you at once.

FOGGERTY (*looking at card*): Malvina de Vere! I don't know Malvina de Vere.

LOTTIE: Oh, that's nonsense. She says you are her dearest friend.

FOGGERTY: Oh, absurd!

LOTTIE: Well, that's what she *says*.

FOGGERTY: The deuce she does! (*Aside:*) Now, this must be someone whom I *should* have known if I hadn't known Spiff – someone, in fact, who's been Spiffed in.* This is awkward. I wonder if Jenny knows of this? (*Aloud:*) By the by, where is Jenny?

LOTTIE: Jenny? Oh, she's upstairs, poor girl.

FOGGERTY (*aside*): 'Poor girl?' Why 'poor girl', I wonder? (*Aloud:*) Ah, poor girl! How is she by this time?

TOTTIE: Oh, pretty well.

FOGGERTY: *Pretty* well? Not very well?

TOTTIE: Why, you can hardly expect her to be very well, on this day of all others.

FOGGERTY: Naturally. (*Aside:*) I wonder what day of all others this is?

LOTTIE: But still, she is as well as can be expected.

FOGGERTY: As well as… (*Aside:*) I see where I am now. I've been married some time, and… I wonder if it's a boy or a girl! It would be ridiculous to ask. I'll go and see her. (*Going.*)

TOTTIE: Where are you going?

FOGGERTY: Going? Why, to see Jenny, of course.

TOTTIE: Oh, you can't possibly see *her* – she's dressing.

FOGGERTY: Well, what of that?

LOTTIE: Upon my word, Mr Foggerty.

TOTTIE: You can't go up to her; you must really wait till she comes down.

FOGGERTY: Oh, she is well enough to come down, is she?

LOTTIE: What a question; and on this day of all others! Of course she is.

FOGGERTY: Exactly; on this day of all others. (*Aside:*) What does she means by 'this day of all others'?

TOTTIE: It's a day *I* never expected to see.

FOGGERTY: Didn't you? Bless me, I knew all about it from the first.

LOTTIE: When one thinks of all the circumstances of the case, one sees how true it is that truth is stranger than fiction.

TOTTIE: Oh, what a novel it would make! Only think. The young and penniless apothecary who had never known what love was—

LOTTIE: The wholesale cheesemonger's daughter—

TOTTIE: Their meeting... the dawn of love in the apothecary's heart—

LOTTIE: The opposition of the cruel and mercenary parent—

TOTTIE: Her determination to wed the apothecary at all hazards—

LOTTIE: Everything at a deadlock! Then the discovery of the pill—

TOTTIE: At midnight—

LOTTIE: Its sudden renown—

TOTTIE: The pill in everybody's mouth—

LOTTIE: Stupendous fortune realised by the inventor in no time. All opposition removed, and they're to be married today!

FOGGERTY (*who has been looking from one to the other in bewildered wonderment during this dialogue*): Today!

LOTTIE: Of course! The successful young apothecary and the cheesemonger's lovely daughter are to be united today.

FOGGERTY (*aside*): Today! (*Aloud:*) But I thought you said she was as well as could be expected?

LOTTIE: Well, so I did, and so she is.

TOTTIE: Bless the man, she's nervous and excited, of course, but she's not too ill to be married.

LOTTIE: I should think *not*, indeed; one must be bad for *that*!

(*Exeunt* LOTTIE *and* TOTTIE, *laughing.*)

FOGGERTY: Then I'm not married after all, and, what's more, I'm to be married today! Why, of course, here's the wedding bouquet! I see it all now. I've invented a pill – the pill's taken – I'm a man of fortune – and the wedding is to take place from my house. Why, with a little tact – a little judicious pumping – how easy it all is. By the by, I wonder where I live? (*Looks out of window.*) Harley Street! Of course it's Harley Street. A man who invents a successful pill always does live in Harley Street! But this lady – my dearest friend on earth; that's awkward – on one's wedding day. I can't imagine anything more awkward – on one's wedding day. Does Jenny know of this? I'll be bound Jenny does *not* know of this. There's something about this lady's method – I don't know what – that convinces me that I shouldn't have told Jenny anything about her. Foggerty, my boy, I'm extremely sorry to say that circumstances point to the fact that you've been going it!

(*Enter* MALVINA DE VERE. *She is a tall, stately lady of middle age and tragical demeanour. She stands at the door for a moment – gazes at him melodramatically – then rushes to his arms.*)

MALVINA: Frederick! At last! At last! (*Gazes at him fondly.*)
FOGGERTY (*aside*): She's a bosom friend – no doubt about that! (*Aloud, and much embarrassed:*) I – a – have much pleasure in—
MALVINA (*gazing at him*): Don't speak, not yet, not yet, I entreat you! Let me drink you in!

FOGGERTY: Certainly. Be so obliging as to say when you've had enough.

MALVINA: There – I'm satisfied.

FOGGERTY (*aside*): I wish *I* was.

MALVINA: Now speak to me! Oh! my love! My tender, tender love! Speak to me as you used to speak to me – call me by the name by which you used to call me!

FOGGERTY: Really… (*Aside:*) By George, I *have* been going it!

MALVINA: The old, old name – the pet name of so many happy memories – oh, call me by it, call me by it!

FOGGERTY: Certainly; I… (*Refers to visiting card.*) I believe I have the – a – pleasure of addressing Miss de Vere?

MALVINA: Miss de Vere! (*Drawing herself back in great surprise.*) Miss de Vere? Why, what means this? Why this extraordinary coolness, why this chilling formality – and on this day of all others?

FOGGERTY: I beg your pardon, but you took me so completely by surprise.

MALVINA: By surprise? Have you forgotten my note, and your reply to it? Read it, sir, read it. (*Gives him a note.*)

FOGGERTY: With very great pleasure. (*Aside:*) Now I shall find out that infernal pet name. (*Reads:*) 'My own.' That's all. (*Disappointed.*) I hate a fellow who calls a girl his 'own'. (*Reads:*) 'I recognise the propriety of your scruples in the particularly delicate relation in which we stand towards each other. But I implore you to come and see me tomorrow morning, nevertheless.' There, you see it says '*tomorrow morning*'.

MALVINA: This *is* tomorrow morning.

FOGGERTY: Nonsense – that can't be; that's ridiculous. (*Refers to note.*) Oh, I see, it was dated yesterday.

MALVINA: And now, sir, before I proceed to that extreme measure to which I have been unhappily so frequently compelled to resort, perhaps you will be so good as to explain and satisfactorily account for the extraordinary coldness of your reception.

FOGGERTY: My coldness? Oh, that was my scrupulous regard for the respect due to you in the particularly delicate relation in which we stand to one another.

MALVINA: It was?

FOGGERTY: It was. Miss de Vere, I find it hard, very hard, to continue this assumption of indifference to you; but I am proud – I am *proud* to say that my better man is triumphant.

MALVINA: I see! I understand it all!

FOGGERTY (*aside*): Then, by George, you've the advantage of me!

MALVINA: You will forgive the undeserved reproaches with which in my jealous madness I dared to assail you?

FOGGERTY: Say no more about them – they are pardoned.

MALVINA: Why, what a mad fool was I!

FOGGERTY: You were – I mean no – not at all. (*Aside:*) I wish she'd go.

MALVINA: But I have been so often the victim of heartless and systematic treachery!

FOGGERTY: Have you?

MALVINA: Why, you know I have.

FOGGERTY: So I do – of course – I know you have! Poor girl, poor girl! When I think of your sad story—

MALVINA: Ah! it *is* a sad story!

FOGGERTY: I know it is. (*Aside:*) *That's* a sad story! (*Aloud:*) But, bless me, it's eleven o'clock, and I've a most important engagement in half an hour, and I'm not dressed. Will you excuse me?

MALVINA: Oh, by all means.

FOGGERTY: I suppose my dressing room's upstairs?

MALVINA: Really, Mr Foggerty, I don't know where your dressing room is!

FOGGERTY: No, of course not. How should you?

MALVINA: Exactly. How should I? But won't you say farewell to me before you go?

FOGGERTY: With great pleasure. But, at the same time, in accordance with the pledge contained in that letter, I must firmly resist the temptation to address you by that old pet name of happy memories, until the relations between us have become more indelicate – that is to say, less delicate than they are.

MALVINA: It is nobly spoken; it is like your heroic self. But you *are* anxious, are you not? You *do* burn with a feverish anxiety to hear the word that is to be spoken this afternoon?

FOGGERTY: Miss de Vere, I assure you, on the honour of a Lancashire Foggerty, that I am tormented with a fidgety anxiety on an infinite number of topics, and on that among others! Good morning. (*Exit.*)

MALVINA: He is gone! How strange and incoherent his manner – how wild and flighty his eye! Oh, mercy on me! can it be that he, too, is false to me? Can it be that I shall be once more driven to resort to the last and hated means of vindicating my rights? No, no – I'll not believe it – and yet… (*Sees breakfast in back room.*) Why, what is this? By the God of Treachery, it is a wedding feast! Whose? Oh, impossible! And yet, his strange embarrassment – his evasive hesitation! Oh, misery – oh, misery, if it should be! Why, what a cursed thing am I! What have I done that this blight should fall on me wherever I go? Why does Infidelity dog my path, while the serpent Treachery lifts his head on high and hisses forth a loud ha! ha! Oh, ye Fate-hags three; soul torturers, my defiance to ye all! The fight is betwixt ye and me, and I am not made of the stuff that yields.

(*Enter* JENNY *in wedding dress, as in Act I.*)

JENNY: There, I think I look lovely! (*Sees* MALVINA:) A lady!

MALVINA (*aside, with emotion*): It is the bride! Down, down, my heart! (*Aloud:*) Fear not, pretty one; I am but Malvina de Vere – a very sorrowful lady.

JENNY: I am sorry you are sorrowful.

MALVINA (*with an effort*): And you – you are the bride in whose honour these festive preparations have been made?

JENNY (*sighing*): Yes, I'm to be married today. How do you like my dress?

MALVINA: It is very well – it is very well. (*Aside:*) How my heart throbs! Down, little one; I must appear calm, and I cannot do so while you beat so rapidly. (*Aloud:*) You – you are about to be married to Mr Foggerty?

JENNY: To Mr Foggerty? Oh dear, no! What could have put such an idea into your head?

MALVINA: You are *not* going to marry Mr Foggerty?

JENNY: Assuredly not! He is my husband's best man!

MALVINA (*relieved*): It is well – it is very well! (*Aside:*) Little heart, you hear?

JENNY: You seem agitated! Can I offer you anything?

MALVINA: I *am* agitated, young bride. I – I can never gaze upon a wedding garb without remembering that I, who am a simple maiden still, might, but for man's perfidy, have been, ere this, a grandmamma.

JENNY: Have they been deceiving you?

MALVINA: Deceiving me? Eighteen times have I stood dauntlessly at matrimony's verge. Eighteen times my coward victim – that is to say, my betrothed – has quailed and fled! He, man in name, blanched at the very danger that I courted.

JENNY: That's so like them! And you, what did you do?

MALVINA: I took the only course that open to me lay. Eighteen times I offered up my bleeding heart a sacrifice at Themis'* sympathetic shrine. Eighteen times did I lay bare its holiest workings, and call on all to come and gaze upon its palpitating pulp. And in each case I recovered substantial damages.

JENNY: You did nobly! And the nineteenth?

MALVINA: His fate is yet uncertain. For many months have I lost sight of him. Yet have I heard within the last few weeks that he is also false and seeks another bride.

JENNY: Oh, poor lady!

MALVINA: It matters little – there's a twentieth in the field, whose exquisitely sensitive regard for my most difficult and delicate position falls scarcely short of the phenomenal; but, ere I yield me to his ardent prayers, I must in honour satisfy myself that my nineteenth is false. This afternoon the problem will be solved.

JENNY: My heart bleeds for you, sad and gentle lady. But whither go you now?

MALVINA: I scarce can say! To wander up and down and to and fro, restless as a caged panther in his den, until the double-barrelled news is brought that I am free to love and bring my action!*

JENNY: Nay, but I'll not consign you to the mercies of the inhospitable street. This is *my* house – or shortly will be so; pray rest you here, and when the solemn ceremony is over, we pray you join our merry-making, and in the wild delirium of the breakfast forget the harrowing trouble at your heart.

MALVINA: I thank you, maiden, for your sympathy. I'll not refuse the shelter that you proffer.

JENNY: You'll find my boudoir on the two-pair-back.* So, for the nonce,* farewell! May Justice pour her balm upon your heart!

MALVINA: She has, my dear, in every other case, and, doubtless, will in this. Once more, farewell. (*Exit.*)

JENNY (*looking after her*): Poor lady, with what a touching dignity she bears her many disappointments! Her sad, sad tale touches me to the heart, for I, too, have loved, but vainly. Oh, how I loved him – and he knew it not! But there – I may not think of *him* – henceforth I may think only of my Theodore!

(*Enter* WALKINSHAW.)

WALKINSHAW: Jenny! My own! At last – at last my own!

JENNY: Oh, Theodore – indifferent to me in all else, but interesting to me inasmuch as I am the only woman who ever kindled the fire of love within your heart, be true to me, be true to me!

WALKINSHAW: Be true to you? While life lasts!

JENNY: And do you love me?

WALKINSHAW: Love you? Haven't I settled the pill upon you?

JENNY: Yes, yes; you have been most generous. I am the only one; am I not?

WALKINSHAW: The only one, in truth.

JENNY: And you have never known the throb of love?

WALKINSHAW: Until you taught it me!

JENNY: It is something; nay, it is much. For you, my Theodore, I have no love, nor have I ever told you that I had; but I esteem you, Theodore, I respect you.

WALKINSHAW: Oh, rapture! But you are sad.

JENNY: Oh, Theodore, a lady has been here – such a sad, sad lady! So tearful yet so calm – so calm and yet so woebegone – so woebegone and yet so dignified! Eighteen times has that poor lady been thrown over.

WALKINSHAW: Thrown over where?

JENNY: And even now she has reason to believe that the nineteenth is trifling with her feelings!

WALKINSHAW (*in great terror*): Bless my soul. What's her name?

JENNY: Her very name is Poetry and Soul!

WALKINSHAW: Oh, then, I don't know her. (*Much relieved.*) It sounds like a firm.

JENNY: She is called Malvina de Vere.

WALKINSHAW (*horrified; aside*): It's she. If she finds me at home, she'll find me out. I'm ruined. (*Aloud:*) Where is she?

JENNY: Sobbing her heart out in the two-pair-back.

WALKINSHAW: In my house?

JENNY: In yours and mine. Poor tortured soul; she waits a wire from her solicitor.

WALKINSHAW (*much agitated*): Jenny, I – I have heard of this lady. She – she is not altogether worthy of your sympathy—

JENNY: What!!! How dare you, sir!

WALKINSHAW: She – she lives on actions for breach. She engages herself to an unsuspecting young man – makes herself intentionally unpleasant. Her lover can't stand her, and breaks it off – and she immediately brings an action.

JENNY: Oh, shame on you to dare in my presence – in the presence of your wife that is to be – to palliate the conduct of a wretch who makes unpleasantness a ground for violating the troth that he has plighted! Oh, shame upon you – shame upon you!

WALKINSHAW: But, Jenny, I—

(*Enter* FOGGERTY *dressed for wedding, and sticking flower in buttonhole.*)

FOGGERTY: There – that's very nice. It's wonderful how a judiciously applied vegetable sets a man off. That'll do, I think. Now if I can only find someone who will give me a clue to… (*Sees* WALKINSHAW*:*) Walkinshaw, my boy, *you* here!

WALKINSHAW: Certainly I am.

FOGGERTY: The very last man I expected to see, I give you my unadulterated word of honour! (*Shaking hands enthusiastically.*)

WALKINSHAW: The last man?

FOGGERTY: The very last, I assure you. I'm more delighted than I can tell you!

WALKINSHAW: Why? It's hardly likely that I should be absent, on this day of all others!

FOGGERTY: Well, it's very friendly of you to say so. I won't forget it, Walkinshaw, depend upon it. Will you take anything? Do! Make yourself at home, you know. This is Liberty Hall. (*Sees* JENNY.) Jenny! at last! My own Jenny! Why, how superb you look, and to think that in half an hour… (*Kisses her.*)

JENNY (*surprised*): Mr Foggerty!

FOGGERTY: And now, tell me how you've been all this time − and what you've been doing − and, in short, tell me all about it.

JENNY: All about what? (*He kisses her.*) Don't!

FOGGERTY: But I must − I'm so happy, so overpoweringly and stupendously happy! (*Kisses her again − she rises, offended.*)

WALKINSHAW (*aside*): I wish Jenny wouldn't let Foggerty kiss her so much; of course it's all right, because they've known each other as children; but still I wish he wouldn't do it! She doesn't let *me*, and I don't see why she should let him.

(FOGGERTY, *who has been paying attention to* JENNY *during this, attempts to kiss her.*)

JENNY: Mr Foggerty, you mustn't, really. I'm astonished at you!

WALKINSHAW: He's overdoing it; upon my soul he is!

FOGGERTY: Pooh, pooh! nonsense; on this day of all others. (*Kisses her again.*)

WALKINSHAW (*aside*): I can't stand this. (*Aloud:*) I say, Foggerty, of course it's all right. I know how you and Jenny are situated – but still I think – I *think*, on this day of all others—

FOGGERTY (*surprised*): What do you mean?

WALKINSHAW: There's too much of it, my boy. I'd leave off if I were you – I would, indeed!

FOGGERTY: No, you wouldn't, Walkinshaw, you jealous dog! (*Aside:*) Poor devil, he hasn't got over his attachment to her yet, and it *is* rather rough on him.

WALKINSHAW: Kissing her under my very nose—

FOGGERTY: Not under *your* very nose – under *her* very nose. Ha! ha! But don't distress yourself, it shan't occur again.

WALKINSHAW: You're overdoing it, my boy.

FOGGERTY: Well, perhaps I am.

WALKINSHAW: I'm sure you are.

FOGGERTY: I agree with you – it's not delicate.

WALKINSHAW: It's d——d indelicate.

FOGGERTY: Yes, on this day of all others!

WALKINSHAW: Exactly, on this day of all others!

FOGGERTY: Then say no more about it. Take one yourself.

WALKINSHAW: Oh, we're in no hurry; *we* can wait.

JENNY (*sighing*): Ah, yes, we can wait!

FOGGERTY: The deuce you can?

WALKINSHAW: Yes; you see, we've plenty of time before us.

JENNY (*sighing*): Plenty!

FOGGERTY (*aside*): Plenty of time before them? Now, what do they mean by *that*?

WALKINSHAW: Well, it's about time we were off. Let's see – are we all here? There's Uncle Fogle and Aunt Bogle for the first carriage, and Lottie and Tottie, and Walker and Balker, and your papa and my mamma – and – yes, we're quite complete. I'll get them all packed off, and then come back for you. (*Exit.*)

FOGGERTY: Jenny, I don't like Walkinshaw's manner.

JENNY: His manner *is* unfortunate, but you mustn't be too hard on him; he's nervous and agitated.

FOGGERTY: I can understand that; but still I don't like it, Jenny, I don't like it.

JENNY: Oh, you *must* make allowance for him, and on this day of all others.

FOGGERTY: Well, poor devil, I suppose he's more to be pitied than blamed.

JENNY: Pitied! Well, I'm sure.

FOGGERTY: Yes, pitied. Now, Jenny, it's no use affecting surprise. I can see as far through a millstone as most people, and, mark my words, that man's in love with you!

JENNY: Of course he is!

FOGGERTY: Oh, you've noticed it?

JENNY (*surprised*): Noticed it? Why, of course I've noticed it!

FOGGERTY: Then I say he's very much to be pitied – he has a dismal prospect before him.

JENNY: Upon my word, Mr Foggerty!

FOGGERTY: Life a blank, every hope crushed, every fond illusion wiped out, nothing before him but a melancholy prime, a blighted sere-and-yellow, and a solitary and desolate old age. Poor Walkinshaw!

JENNY: How dare you say these things to me?

FOGGERTY: Eh?

JENNY: I say how dare you? From this moment I devote myself, heart and soul, to his happiness; it shall be my only care, my only thought!

FOGGERTY: The devil you will!

JENNY: I will, I swear it! It will be my duty, and my duty I will do!

FOGGERTY: It seems to me that you take an exceedingly comprehensive view of your duty! Look here, Jenny; let's understand one another. (*Sits by her, puts his arm round her waist.*) I know you're as good a girl as ever stepped. Still—

JENNY: Frederick – Mr Foggerty – you mustn't!

FOGGERTY: Mustn't what?

JENNY: Put your arm round my waist.

FOGGERTY: Well, it *is* round your waist.

JENNY (*struggling*): But I say you mustn't.

FOGGERTY: Why not? Walkinshaw can't see.

JENNY: That has nothing to do with it. I won't allow it, because it's not right – on this day of all others!

FOGGERTY: Indeed? I should have thought if ever there *was* a day on which I might be permitted to take such an innocent freedom, this day of all others is the day.

JENNY (*crying*): How dare you say such things to me! It is most unkind to me, and most unfair to your friend.

FOGGERTY: My friend? Oh, Walkinshaw! I tell you he can't see.

JENNY: I don't care, it's most unfair to him.

FOGGERTY: It seems to me you've a remarkably tender regard for Walkinshaw's feelings!

JENNY: Certainly I have. As you know, I don't pretend that I love him.

FOGGERTY: Well, I should hope not!

JENNY: I mean as a wife is expected to love her husband.

FOGGERTY: Yes, that's what *I* mean!

JENNY: Yet I have a sincere regard for him, and, be assured of this, I shall always respect his privileges.

FOGGERTY: Upon my word, ma'am, situated as I am—

JENNY: Yes, I know, you were my childhood's friend; but that only makes it all the more dreadful, and sincerely as I esteem *you*, I must tell you at once that if ever you presume to attempt the slightest, very slightest, familiarity with me, except in Mr Walkinshaw's presence, I shall give directions that you are never to be admitted into the house again!

FOGGERTY (*utterly aghast*): But, Jenny, listen for one moment.

JENNY: It's useless, Frederick. It's best to begin as we mean to go on.

FOGGERTY: Oh! Don't you think you'd better *marry* Walkinshaw at once?

JENNY: Yes, we shall be too late if we don't start very soon.

FOGGERTY (*furious*): I say, don't you think you'd better marry Walkinshaw – *Walkinshaw* – at once?

JENNY: I say yes, I do. I can't imagine what's detaining him.

FOGGERTY (*bewildered*): Jenny! Jenny! (*Suddenly:*) Great Heavens! (*Springs horrified to his feet.*)

JENNY: What's the matter? You are ill – some water – quick – quick!

FOGGERTY (*gasping*): Jenny – attend to me! Am I to understand that you are really – going – to – marry Walkinshaw?

(*During this she has loosened his necktie, and dabbed a wet handkerchief on his temples, as he leans tottering against a table.*)

JENNY: How can you ask such a ridiculous question?

FOGGERTY: No, but are you? Answer me, yes or no. Are you?

JENNY: Am I? You know I am.

FOGGERTY (*overpowered*): You are?

JENNY: Of course; don't be absurd.

FOGGERTY (*wildly*): But don't marry him! For Heaven's sake don't marry him! Jenny, you shan't, you can't! I won't stand by and see it done! (*Sobbing:*) Oh, Jenny, Jenny, whom I love so deeply!

JENNY: Mr Foggerty, you amaze me!

FOGGERTY (*surprised*): Amaze you? Why, you know I love you!

JENNY: I? Indeed, I know nothing of the kind!

FOGGERTY: Why, I've told you over and over again!

JENNY: You have told *me* so? Never!

FOGGERTY: How can you say that? Didn't I propose, and didn't you accept me, and weren't we engaged, and – stop. No, no. (*Aside:*) I'm mixing it all up again!

JENNY (*in blank astonishment*): Oh, you must have dreamt all this!

FOGGERTY: Exactly, that's it. I must have dreamt it. But did I *never* tell you that I loved you?

JENNY (*weeping*): Oh no, no, no. Why didn't you? Why didn't you?

FOGGERTY: I don't know. I – I suppose I forgot to mention it.

JENNY (*wildly*): Oh, if I had only known – if I had only known!

FOGGERTY (*excitedly*): Then – you loved me?

JENNY (*horrified*): What have I said?

FOGGERTY: You did! You do! You can't deny it! You shan't deny it! You loved me, madly, passionately – how could you help it?

JENNY: Frederick – in mercy spare me! It is cruel, cruel to say such things to me, just as I am on the point of marrying another man!

FOGGERTY: But *don't* marry another man! He's unworthy of you – I'm not! I love you desperately – he doesn't! I'll do so all my life – he won't! He *can* live without you – I can't! I *shall* go mad if you don't have me – he shan't! Tell Walkinshaw to go and hang himself – he won't mind – he's a good-natured fellow, and he'll do it, if you say it's for me.

JENNY: Impossible! I could not tell him to go and do that. Oh, it is too late – too late! Oh, Frederick, why, *why* didn't you tell me this before?

FOGGERTY (*wildly*): I don't know! There's my difficulty! Situated as I am, it's impossible to say. I thought I had. But it seems I hadn't. No doubt there's a reason for it if one only knew what it was – but one don't! I hope I'm clear?

JENNY (*drying her eyes*): Not very, but anyway, it is too late now. The clergyman is at this moment waiting impatiently to unite me to Theodore Walkinshaw. I regard him with a wondering respect as one whose heart had never throbbed with love until I taught it to. But *love* him? No! I do not love him! After what you have elicited from me it would be worse than affectation to deny that my heart has long been yours, and, but for your unaccountable silence, we might have been happy. As it is, Frederick, we must never, never meet again. I embark on my married life with a bruised and broken heart. Farewell, for ever! (*Exit.*)

FOGGERTY (*wildly*): Jenny, Jenny, come back! Gone, gone from me for ever! To be knitted to Walkinshaw; and the poor child is fond of me, has been for years, ever since we were children! What was I about not to have seen it? Why didn't I tell her I adored her? That's just where it is! I don't know! I haven't the ghost of an idea! I see it all now! If I had never known Spiff, I should never have bolted from her to Jenny – never have interfered with Walkinshaw, whose courtship would have gone on swimmingly, and culminated in matrimony, as it's going to do today. And all this heart-breaking misery, this preposterous coupling of ill-assorted souls, this whirling chaos of discord-ant sympathies, is the consequence of the ill-omened matrimonial arrangements of Colonel Culpepper's favourite dog's father! (*Throws himself on sofa, and bur-ies his head in pillow.*)

(*Enter* WALKINSHAW *and* OLD TALBOT.)

TALBOT: Come, come, *are* we all ready? Then let's be off. Where's Foggerty?

WALKINSHAW: Foggerty? Oh, here he is, on the sofa.

TALBOT: What's the matter with him! Isn't he well?

WALKINSHAW (*aside to* TALBOT): Well, the fact is, I lost my temper with him just now, and it's upset him, but I'll make it all right. (*Goes to him.*) Foggerty, my boy, come, come, cheer up, I didn't mean to speak unkindly to you; but really—

FOGGERTY (*without turning round*): Oh, go, sir, go!

WALKINSHAW: Come, come, be reasonable, if *you* caught a fellow kissing the girl you loved – what would you do?

FOGGERTY (*wildly*): What would I do? Shall I show you what I would do? I'd fly at him. Thus! (*Flying at* WALKINSHAW.) I'd shake him – thus! (*Shaking him violently, and driving him down to proscenium.*) I'd throttle him – thus! (*Knocks him about wildly,* WALKINSHAW *quite limp and helpless in his hands.*) I'd say, 'Give her back to me, you traitor! You double-dyed villain! You slayer of hopes! You assassin of hearts!' There! (*Flinging him violently on the stage.*) That's what I'd do!

WALKINSHAW (*all of a heap and breathless on the floor, and much disordered in dress*): I see, thank you! I – I think you would be justified.

TALBOT: Dear! dear! (*Helping* WALKINSHAW *up, and re-arranging his hair and cravat:*) Foggerty, this is not pretty behaviour towards a bridegroom on his wedding day!

FOGGERTY: Pretty behaviour! And you, infamous old traitor. Would you like to see what I would do to a scheming father who first gives me his daughter and then hands her over to somebody else? (*Shaking him violently.*)

TALBOT (*bewildered*): It would be interesting, of course. Perhaps if you illustrated on Walkinshaw I should see it better than if you did it to me.

(*All three with their costumes and hair very much disarranged.*)

FOGGERTY: Walkinshaw! After all I have done for him, to rob me of the only girl I ever loved!

TALBOT: You loved my girl?

WALKINSHAW: Did you love Jenny?

FOGGERTY (*sarcastically*): Did I love Jenny? Do you think I should have been engaged to her if I hadn't?

TALBOT: Engaged to her!

FOGGERTY: Engaged to her? Yes! Oh, I forgot; that's all been Spiffed out! I've been mixing again!

TALBOT: Upon my soul I think you have! And pretty freely too!

FOGGERTY: There, don't mind me; don't take any notice of what I say! Give me air, or I shall choke! (*Staggers on to balcony.*)

TALBOT *and* WALKINSHAW (*together*): I say, doesn't it strike you—

TALBOT: I beg your pardon—

WALKINSHAW: I beg yours.

TALBOT: After you!

WALKINSHAW: Not at all!

TALBOT: I was going to say, doesn't it strike you that there's something very incoherent in Foggerty's manner?

WALKINSHAW: The very thing I was going to say to you!

TALBOT: Mark my words; he's mad!

WALKINSHAW: Staring mad!

TALBOT: It's an awful thing!

WALKINSHAW: Appalling!

TALBOT: Glass of wine?

WALKINSHAW: With pleasure!

(*They take wine together. Enter* JENNY.)

JENNY: Stop!

TALBOT: But we can't be always stopping – what's the matter now?

JENNY: This wedding – it must not take place!

TALBOT *and* WALKINSHAW (*together*): Mustn't take place!

WALKINSHAW: Jenny, what in the world do you mean?

JENNY: Stand off, sir! Do not dare to approach me! I regard you with contempt and loathing unutterable.

TALBOT *and* WALKINSHAW (*together*): Jenny!

JENNY: Approach me not, I say! You have trifled with my most sacred feelings! You have outraged my tenderest sensibilities. I regard you as a snaky and systematic serpent – and thus – and thus – I extricate myself from your slimy toils. (*Tears license.*)

TALBOT: Oh, Jenny, Jenny, this is not pretty behaviour to your husband on his wedding day!

JENNY: Pretty behaviour! Do you know that man?

TALBOT: Know him? Yes, very well!

JENNY: You know his smooth and plausible outside – but his inside – do you know *that*?

TALBOT: Really, my dear, I'm not his medical attendant; but what has he done?

JENNY: Unhinged and unstrung by the prospects of the approaching ceremony, I sought just now the congenial sympathy of the sad, sad lady on the second floor. As I approached her room I saw the door ajar – she was in close communion with her solicitor.

(WALKINSHAW *much agitated.*)

I heard his voice – and thus – and thus he spoke: 'Console yourself, oh, sad, sad lady, for we have evidence that Walkinshaw – the fickle, fluttering, faithless Walkinshaw – is on the eve of marriage to another!' It was enough – too much – I cared to hear no more!

TALBOT: Dear me, Walkinshaw, I am surprised at you!

WALKINSHAW: But, Jenny, hear me.

JENNY: I will hear nothing. It is enough for me that you have loved. Henceforward to me you are as one that is dead! You are an obliterated postage stamp – not the less obliterated because the die has been wielded by an unworthy hand. Happily, Truth, Honour, Rectitude, Morality, Propriety, Benevolence, Veneration and First Love are on the Balcony. They meet in Frederick, and to him I confide my heart!

(FOGGERTY *enters from balcony.*)

FOGGERTY: Jenny! I was sure you would! I was sure that when you came to think it over you couldn't help it. But, Walkinshaw?

JENNY: He is dead.

FOGGERTY: That's very sudden.

JENNY: He is dead to me. He lives to drag on a miserable existence, as a depressed and degraded monster.

FOGGERTY: I'm shocked at you, Walkinshaw!

WALKINSHAW: Miss Talbot, I *cannot* struggle against your determination. I know that when you say you will not marry me you mean it!

FOGGERTY: She did last time.

TALBOT: Eh?

FOGGERTY: Oh, nothing, nothing.

WALKINSHAW: I have only to ask that in memory of what I once was to you, you will keep my unhappy secret, and not subject me to the hideous consequences of an exposure.

JENNY: Sir, you deserve no mercy; but I am merciful. Your shameful secret is safe with me.

FOGGERTY: Walkinshaw, I'm at a loss for words in which to express definitely my sense of your infamous conduct, because I am not at present acquainted with the nature of your offence.

TALBOT: But, Jenny, you can't marry this man – he's mad! He can't contract matrimony – it would be illegal!

JENNY: They say you are mad, my own! Is it because you have never loved before?

FOGGERTY: Heed them not. They mistake the desponding utterings of a crushed heart for the maniacal ravings of an unseated brain!

(UNCLE FOGLE *and* TALBOT *both about to speak at once.*)

TALBOT: I beg your pardon.

FOGLE: I beg yours.

TALBOT: Not at all.

FOGLE: Go on.

TALBOT: I was going to say that we must get a Commission*
  to sit on him.
FOGLE: Just what I was going to say.
TALBOT: It's a pitiable circumstance.
FOGLE: Horrible!
TALBOT: Deplorable!
FOGLE: Disastrous!
TALBOT: Glass of wine?
FOGLE: With pleasure.

(*They drink together.*)

JENNY (*coming down with* FOGGERTY): My own, own love!
  Mine, and only mine! Oh, tell me again you, at least,
  have never loved before!
FOGGERTY: Never! Often have I lain awake at night wondering what manner of thing this love of which I had
  heard so much might be, and now the sun has risen
  on my darkness, and all seems clear as summer noon!
JENNY: My love! Oh, this is ecstasy!

(*During this,* TALBOT *and* WALKINSHAW *and others have
been warily approaching* JENNY *and* FOGGERTY: TALBOT
and WALKER *seize* JENNY, *while* WALKINSHAW, UNCLE
FOGLE, *and* BALKER *seize* FOGGERTY. *The lovers are torn
asunder.*)

FOGGERTY: Unhand me, villains!
JENNY: Frederick, my own! They are taking me from you!
FOGGERTY: Cowards! Thus and thus do I deal with ye!

(FOGGERTY *throws them off.* JENNY *breaks from* TALBOT. *They rush to one another, and embrace.*)

JENNY: Who shall separate us now? I am my own mistress!
FOGGERTY: And mine!

(*Enter* MALVINA. JENNY *rushes to her, and clings round her neck.* WALKINSHAW, *seeing her, buries his head in a newspaper to escape recognition.*)

MALVINA: Frederick, rejoice with me! The news, the great and glorious tidings, have arrived! My faithless lover *is* on the point of marriage with another, and I am at last free to accept those professions of affection with which for the last twelve months you have so eloquently pleaded, for my hand!

(JENNY *recoils in horror from her. Turns and looks at* FOGGERTY, *then faints in* TALBOT*'s arms.* FOGGERTY *stands confused for a moment, then turns round, rushes wildly to balcony at the back of the stage and leaps out into the street. The others rush after him to stop him, but they are too late.* MALVINA *faints in the arms of* WALKINSHAW, *whose head is still wrapped up in a newspaper.*)

PICTURE

ACT III

SCENE

Parlour in WALKINSHAW*'s house, night. Lamps lit. The general arrangement of the scene is the same as the scene of* TALBOT*'s house in Act I.* WALKINSHAW *and* TALBOT *discovered.*

WALKINSHAW: This is a dismal night, to what was to have been a fellow's wedding day.

TALBOT: It might be more cheerful. But take heart, be sanguine. Perhaps you and Jenny would not have got on. You're not a very nice man, you know.

WALKINSHAW: No, I know I'm not, but it's rather hard that my having been once engaged to Malvina de Vere should cause Jenny to break off with me at the last moment. And for Foggerty, who has also fallen into that middle-aged harpy's toils.

TALBOT: Don't mind Foggerty. Jenny won't have him now. I have got evidence that he is stark, staring mad, and, between ourselves, I have applied for a Commission *de lunatico** to sit on him at once. I am going to make the appointment now.

WALKINSHAW: Hadn't you better wait till he comes back?

TALBOT: Hasn't he come back?

WALKINSHAW: No, it's eight hours since he took his leap from the balcony, and nobody has seen him since.

71

TALBOT: Dear me! I don't think he could have hurt himself seriously, for I saw him flying down the street, ten miles an hour, with Malvina after him. (*Looking out of window:*) Here he is – he has jumped out of a four-wheeler, which is tearing down the street at full speed. And there is another four-wheeler tearing full speed after it. What can it mean?

(*Enter* FOGGERTY, *exhausted. Dress muddy and disordered, hair dishevelled. He throws himself into a chair, breathless.*)

FOGGERTY: At last! Safe at last.

WALKINSHAW: Why, where have you been?

FOGGERTY: Everywhere.

TALBOT: You seem rather out of breath.

FOGGERTY: I am a little.

TALBOT: A glass of wine?

FOGGERTY: With pleasure. (*Helps himself to a glass of sherry, and drinks.*)

WALKINSHAW: And where is Malvina?

FOGGERTY: I have given her the slip at last. When I left the house I bolted up Harley Street. Malvina followed. I got into a cab; she got into another. I said, 'Drive anywhere.' He drove everywhere. I told him to drive like the devil. He drove like the devil. So did Malvina. Regent's Park, Primrose Hill, Kentish Town, Holloway, Ball's Pond, Dalston, Hackney, Old Ford, Bow, Whitechapel, London Bridge, Southwark. At Southwark my horse fainted; so did Malvina's. I jumped out – got another cab. So did Malvina. Off again, Old Kent Road, Peckham,

Camberwell, Walworth, Kennington, Brixton, Clapham, Battersea, Wandsworth. At Wandsworth my horse fainted. So did Malvina's. Jumped out, but no cab to be found. Bolted, on foot, followed by Malvina; ran through Putney, Barnes, Mortlake, Kew, Chiswick, Turnham Green, Shepherd's Bush, Kensal Green, Malvina after me. At Kensal Green I fainted; so did Malvina. Off again, through West-bourne Park. At Westbourne Park I found a cab; so did Malvina. Off again; Maida Hill, Edgware Road, St John's Wood, New Road, Harley Street. As I passed the door, jumped out unobserved, and left my empty cab tearing on ten miles an hour, and Malvina after it.

TALBOT: Aren't you tired after your stroll?

FOGGERTY: A little.

TALBOT: I am not surprised. Will you excuse me, I have a business appointment. (*Aside to* WALKINSHAW:) Don't let him go; keep him here till I return. (*Exit.*)

WALKINSHAW: That is a very determined woman.

FOGGERTY: A woman of singular strength of character.

WALKINSHAW (*anxiously*): Do you think there is any chance of her coming here?

FOGGERTY: Not the remotest. (*Knock heard.*) There she is.

WALKINSHAW (*aside*): Malvina here! She must not catch me. (*Aloud:*) Foggerty, you'll keep my secret – you'll not betray me?

FOGGERTY: Not for worlds.

WALKINSHAW: A thousand thanks. I will never forget it. (*Shakes his hand and exit.*)

FOGGERTY: I don't know what your secret is, but it's quite safe with me. There she is – it's no use, I can't go any further, fairly run to earth! (*Throws himself into chair to right of stage.*)

(*Enter* MALVINA *from left, breathless and much tumbled. She throws herself into a chair to left of stage.*)

FOGGERTY: Good evening.
MALVINA: Good evening.
FOGGERTY: London is a large city.
MALVINA: Enormous.
FOGGERTY: Capital cabs, though.
MALVINA: Capital cabs.
FOGGERTY: Didn't I catch sight of you in Southwark this afternoon?
MALVINA: Quite possible.
FOGGERTY: I thought it was you.
MALVINA: It was. Going to marry me?
FOGGERTY: No.
MALVINA: Don't you love me?
FOGGERTY: Not that I am aware of.
MALVINA: But you proposed to me.
FOGGERTY: I have no recollection of it.
MALVINA: I have got it in writing over and over again.
   (*Produces a bundle of letters.*)
FOGGERTY: All those mine?
MALVINA: Every man jack of them.
FOGGERTY: May I look at them?
MALVINA: Not exactly – wasn't born yesterday.
FOGGERTY (*aside*): No, you certainly were *not*.

MALVINA: You're quite resolved?

FOGGERTY: Quite. You must conquer this passion. I am sorry if I have encouraged hopes which are not destined to be realised; but, although I have a sincere regard for you, I can never be more to you than a friend.

MALVINA: That is your ultimatum?

FOGGERTY: That is my ultimatum.

MALVINA: Then again I have to resort to that dread expedient which a sympathetic country has provided for the unsuspecting victims of man's designing villainy. Allow me.

(*Gives paper to* FOGGERTY.)

FOGGERTY: What's this?

MALVINA: It is a writ of summons at the suit of Malvina de Vere, spinster, against Frederick Foggerty, bachelor, to recover damages for breach of promise to marry.

FOGGERTY: Thank you. The damages, I see, are not stated.

MALVINA: Not yet. True delicacy shrinks from placing matters of this quasi-sentimental character upon a mere business footing. I thought it would be altogether more delicate if we could arrive at an estimate by a friendly calculation.

FOGGERTY: Very thoughtful.

MALVINA: It's a pretty idea; I always do it. Now, let me see. First of all there is my distress of mind, and consequent wear and tear of personal beauty.

FOGGERTY: Not worth naming. Miss de Vere is, if possible, more lovely than ever.

MALVINA: Yes, I know I am now; but oh! think, think of the anxious days and sleepless nights yet to come!

FOGGERTY: To be sure.

MALVINA: The worm in the bud—*

FOGGERTY: True; I forgot the worm in the bud. How long do you think you will be before you get over it?

MALVINA: It generally takes about six weeks.

FOGGERTY: That is not very long.

MALVINA: Make it months if you like.

FOGGERTY: Not for worlds. You think the worm will have had enough in six weeks?

MALVINA: Oh, I think so. Six weeks at a guinea a day – forty-two guineas.

FOGGERTY: Dear!

MALVINA: I couldn't do it for less.

FOGGERTY (*getting his arm round her*): Make it pounds, do.*

MALVINA: What a wheedling way you have! Very well, pounds. Then there is the disappointment, the blackness of a desolate future. What shall we say for the disappointment?

FOGGERTY: I shouldn't put that at a high figure if I were you. I shouldn't make a good husband.

MALVINA (*politely*): Oh, I won't allow that for a moment.

FOGGERTY: No, but indeed I shouldn't.

MALVINA (*insinuatingly*): Not even such a wife as I?

FOGGERTY: If anything could make a domestic man of me it would be the knowledge that I had a nice, snug, cosy creature like you waiting at home for me; but nothing could.

MALVINA: I don't think I could put the disappointment at less than a hundred.

FOGGERTY: A hundred! A hundred for such a good-for-nothing scamp as I? Ridiculous! It's absurd. You don't know what a ruffian I am. Fifty is the outside figure.

MALVINA: Oh, Mr Foggerty, you under-rate yourself. I don't think – stand up.

(*He stands up.*)

No, I couldn't put the disappointment at less than a hundred.

FOGGERTY: Fifty!

MALVINA: A hundred!

FOGGERTY: Split the difference, and say seventy-five.

MALVINA: Very well; but it's a positive insult to you to put it so low.

FOGGERTY: Don't mention it, I beg.

MALVINA: Then we come to the publicity of the thing – the shame of having to lay bare in open court the holiest feelings of our imperfect nature.

FOGGERTY: Haven't you got used to that yet?

MALVINA: Used to it? My dear Mr Foggerty, believe me, that the agony of having to trot out one's affections for the entertainment of a ribald public becomes more excruciating each time. On the whole, I cannot quote the publicity at a lower figure than five hundred.

FOGGERTY: Four.

MALVINA: Five.

FOGGERTY: Split the difference, and say four hundred and fifty. Come, now, do, for me.

MALVINA: It's ridiculously cheap; but I never did in all my experience come across anybody with such coaxing ways. But then, there's the trousseau.

FOGGERTY: But that will do for next time. I suppose you have had the same trousseau in each case.

MALVINA: Oh dear, no! Only the last four cases. I find that a trousseau only lasts out six engagements. You see, it gets handled and messed. And there's the moth and change of fashion. I usually reckon it at twenty-five per cent off prime cost. Prime cost two hundred – twenty-five off that – one-fifty.

FOGGERTY: How much is that altogether?

MALVINA: Let's see. Six hundred and seventeen pounds. Then there are costs as between lawyer and client.

FOGGERTY: Say six hundred, all told, and then – who knows – perhaps we shall be engaged again.

MALVINA: Oh, I couldn't do it. First-class evidence, you know, warm and flowery letters – all in your own writing.

FOGGERTY: Are they warm and flowery?

MALVINA: Ridiculously so. There's poetry in some of them – your own.

FOGGERTY (*aside*): My own! I wonder where I got it from? (*Aloud:*) But wait a moment, Jenny won't have me now. I really don't see what is to prevent me marrying you.

MALVINA: Nothing whatever, if you prefer that course; then there will only be the costs out of pocket.

FOGGERTY: There's the remains of a fine woman about you.

MALVINA: I am generally known as the Splendid Ruin.

FOGGERTY: You *are* a splendid ruin – a sprig or two of ivy and an owl under your arm and you would be complete. My dear girl, if it is a question of paying six hundred pounds and costs, or marrying you, I'll marry you.

MALVINA: You will?

FOGGERTY: Certainly. I must have seen something in you, or I shouldn't have proposed to you. I have no doubt you are a much more agreeable woman than you look.

MALVINA: Surely, surely, you know how agreeable I am by this time.

FOGGERTY: Yes – yes – no doubt; but – Malvina—

MALVINA: Call me by the old pet name – the name of happy memories.

FOGGERTY: Yes – that is just it – I don't know what it was.

MALVINA (*astonished*): You don't know what it was?

FOGGERTY: Malvina, I will be candid with you. A singular misfortune has overtaken me – my mind, perfectly keen and sound at the present moment, is a blank as regards everything that took place before this morning – my memory is quite gone.

MALVINA: How remarkable!

FOGGERTY: Odd, isn't it?

MALVINA: Then that accounts—

FOGGERTY: For my not knowing that confounded pet name of happy memories, and fifty other things. Now, if you will undertake to tell me all about myself – who I am, what I am, where I am, and who and what everybody else is – and, in short, enable me to hold my position before the world without making an infernal fool of myself, I'll marry you out of gratitude. Now, is it a bargain?

MALVINA: Is it a bargain? I rather think it is a bargain. But what an extraordinary state of things.

FOGGERTY: Well, it is singular. I'll just run upstairs and make a change. You see what a state I am in after my run; and then the sooner you post me up to this morning the better.

MALVINA: I will; go, my love, and in the mean time I will draw up a statement of facts for your information. Farewell.

FOGGERTY: Farewell. Don't you think—

MALVINA: Think what?

FOGGERTY: That under the circumstances I might venture to – no – better not. (*Exit.*)

MALVINA: At last, oh Fate, thou smilest on me! There seems some prospect that that blighted bud, my heart, may blossom into wedded dignity. But who are these who break my solitude?

(*Enter* TALBOT, *followed by* DOCTOR LOBB, DOCTOR DOBB *and* BLOGG, *a rough, sullen-looking man, who keeps in the background.*)

TALBOT: Come in, gentlemen, pray. Be so good as to sit down. (*Sees* MALVINA.) Oh! the athletic lady. I beg your pardon, Mr Foggerty—

MALVINA: Has sought the sacred precincts of his chamber, to make a certain change in his apparel.

TALBOT: Oh! exactly – he has had a fatiguing afternoon. (*Aside:*) Dear me, this is awkward.

MALVINA: I'll not intrude upon your converse, sirs. I wait an interview with Frederick, and will, with your permission, gentlemen, attend his coming in the two-pair-back. (*Curtseys and exit.*)

TALBOT: Fine woman, sound in wind and limb. (*Aloud:*) Gentlemen, the unfortunate subject of your investigation will be here in a very few minutes. You will not find him violent, gentlemen.

DR LOBB: His paroxysms are mild, are they?

TALBOT: I should hardly call them paroxysms – they don't amount to that; I should rather describe him as the victim of extraordinary hallucinations.

DR DOBB: Very sad indeed.

DR LOBB: And what, my dear Mr Talbot, is the subject or bent of his delusions?

TALBOT: Well, gentlemen, among other singular misconceptions he is under the impression that he is the inventor of the famous Longevity Pill.

DR DOBB: Pardon me – the 'notorious' – we don't use the term 'famous' in connection with patent medicines. We call them 'notorious'.

TALBOT: Oh! then he thinks he invented the 'notorious' Longevity Pill.

DR LOBB: It is a very significant symptom. I remember the case of an unfortunate man who systematically infringed other people's patents, and actually made a fine fortune by doing so – mad, sir – hopelessly mad.

TALBOT: He also believes that he derives a very large income by its sale, when in point of fact he has not a penny in the world.

DR DOBB: Oh, a very common delusion. I recollect an instance of a poor half-witted creature who drew enormous cheques on a bank at which he had positively no account whatever, and in a name which actually did not belong to him. The cheques were cashed and he was off to America before the delusion was discovered. Mad, sir – quite mad.

TALBOT: Then again, he will accept any theory concerning himself that you choose to suggest. You can make him believe that he is a soldier, sailor, tinker, tailor, plough-boy, apothecary, thief – all in turn. Remarkable, isn't it?

DR LOBB: Not at all. Nothing more common. I once gave evidence in the case of an unhappy man, who obtained large sums of money from charitable people on the plea that he was a bricklayer's widow with twelve children. The poor fellow would have had twelve months' imprisonment with hard labour but for my evidence. Mad, sir, hopelessly mad.

TALBOT: If you will excuse me for a moment, gentlemen, I will send him to you. You will find the sherry on the sideboard. (*Aside:*) Clear-headed, logical men of sense, these mad doctors. (*Exit.*)

DR DOBB (*turning to* BLOGG): Now, Blogg.

BLOGG: Sir.

DR DOBB: Attend to us.

DR LOBB: Dr Dobb means listen attentively to what we say.

DR DOBB: If we find it necessary, as no doubt we shall, to give this unfortunate gentleman into your charge, you will humour him in everything.

DR LOBB: Dr Dobb means you will contradict him in nothing.

DR DOBB: In nothing whatever.

DR LOBB: In other words, in nothing at all.

BLOGG: All right, guv'nor.

DR DOBB: Now, mind you keep your eye upon him.

DR LOBB: In other words, don't let him get out of your sight.

DR DOBB: Whatever he says, accept his delusion.

DR LOBB: My friend means, humour his hallucinations.

DR DOBB: Agree to his statements at once, however absurd they may seem.

DR LOBB: In other words, accept his theories, however ridiculous they may appear.

(*During this* BLOGG *is sitting, eating.*)

DR DOBB: It's the only way to deal with a confirmed delusionist.

DR LOBB: There is no other course to take with a hopeless visionary.

(*Enter* FOGGERTY, *unobserved.*)

DR DOBB: And now we had better go and prepare our report.

DR LOBB: By all means. (*Going.*)

DR DOBB (*politely*): After you.

DR LOBB: Couldn't think of it.

DR DOBB: Oh, but I insist.

DR LOBB: As you please. (*Exit.*)

DR DOBB: D——d coxcomb. (*Following.*)

FOGGERTY (*who has been staring at the* DOCTORS *in blank astonishment during this dialogue, turns to* BLOGG, *who is eating impassively*): Now, what is this? Is it alive, or is it stuffed?

BLOGG (*finishing his supper*): I'm stuffed.

FOGGERTY: What are you doing here?

BLOGG: I'm keeping a eye on you.

FOGGERTY: Do I understand that your instructions are to follow me wherever I go?

BLOGG: No, cause you ain't agoing nowhere.

FOGGERTY (*aside*): Now, how am I to deal with this ruffian? I could kick him out – at least, I think I could – but he seems to have some right here – he isn't a man in possession! (*Aloud:*) You aren't a man in possession, are you?

BLOGG: No, I ain't a man in possession.

FOGGERTY (*suddenly*): I see what it is – he's a constable. I have committed a crime, which I shouldn't have committed if Spiff hadn't been Spiffed out. And these two black-and-white scoundrels are detect-ives. (*Aloud:*) I say, those two piebald idiots who left as I came in are detectives – you can't deny that!

BLOGG (*stolidly*): I ain't agoin' to deny nothin'.

FOGGERTY (*aside*): This is perfectly appalling! What have I done? What is my crime? Is it embezzlement, forgery, bigamy, highway robbery – what? That's it, I haven't an idea.

BLOGG: Don't take on so, there's lots in the same fix.

FOGGERTY: Lots in the same fix! Yes, I know there are; but they know what they've done, I don't. (*Suddenly:*) Walkinshaw is at the bottom of this.

BLOGG: Ah! Walkinshaw's at the bottom of it!

FOGGERTY: Of course he is. He has led me into this; mind, whatever it is, he has led me into it!

BLOGG: Ah! he's led you into it.

FOGGERTY: Whatever it is, I will confess all. I will turn Queen's evidence against Walkinshaw, and will bring Walkinshaw to justice; and, in return for my services to the State, claim the Royal Pardon.

BLOGG: Ah, that is your game! Nothing like it!

FOGGERTY: Now you, sir, just attend carefully to what I say. I intend to make a clean breast of it and admit everything. (*Aside:*) It would simplify matters if I had some remote notion, just a vague, distant, glimmering of an idea, what Walkinshaw and I have done. Never mind: half a dozen shrewdly framed leading questions will pump it all out. (*Aloud:*) Now, then, are you ready to receive my confession?

BLOGG: All right – fire away.

FOGGERTY (*aloud*): Now, then, you know, of course, *when* this deed was done, for which Walkinshaw and I will shortly have to answer to the outraged majesty of the law? (*Waits anxiously for the reply.*)

BLOGG (*indifferently*): Oh, I know – fust of April.

FOGGERTY (*seizing on the idea*): On the very first day of April, in the year of grace 1879, this deed for which Walkinshaw and I will shortly have to answer to the outraged majesty of the law was perpetrated. We selected the first of April because – because we were anxious to get it over as soon after March as possible. Now, then, when do you think we did it?

BLOGG (*stupidly*): Can't say, I'm sure.

FOGGERTY: No; but guess.

BLOGG: I ain't good at guessin'.

FOGGERTY (*aside*): What an unimaginative ass it is. (*Aloud:*) Come, now, make an effort – just one.

BLOGG (*after a pause*): Twelve o'clock at night – when nobody was lookin'.

FOGGERTY: At the mystic hour of midnight, on the very first day of April, in the year of grace 1879, Walkinshaw and I, having previously ascertained that we were secure from the impertinent observation of casual passers-by, perpetrated that deed, for which we shall only too surely have to take our stand at the bar of the outraged majesty of the law. We selected midnight because it's generally darker then than it is in the daylight. Well, there I was. There I was, I say. I say I was there.

BLOGG: Alone?

FOGGERTY: Alone in the grim and ghostly solitude of that April midnight. I needn't tell you how I was occupied.

BLOGG: Maybe you was digging a hole?

FOGGERTY: Armed with a pickaxe and a spade, stripped to the shirt, and with the beady dews of mental agony upon my brow, I shovelled up the fat, black earth until the hole was wide and deep enough for – for the purpose we had in view. Scarcely had I satisfied myself that the hole was wide and deep enough for the purpose we had in view when… what do you think happened?

BLOGG: P'r'aps Walkinshaw came up?

FOGGERTY: Creeping guiltily in the ghostly moonlight, as one whose mind was burdened with a crime too great for him to bear, Walkinshaw came up. You know as well as I do what that monster in human form had with him.

BLOGG: Maybe it was a sack?

FOGGERTY: It *was* a sack. Closed up at one end but open at the other for the convenience of removing whatever it was intended to contain. You see, I am perfectly candid. I conceal nothing from you. That sack contained – the booty.

BLOGG: Oh! she was a booty, was she?

FOGGERTY: Eh?

BLOGG: I say she was a booty, was she?

FOGGERTY: She? Did you say 'she'?

BLOGG: You said she was a booty!

FOGGERTY (*recovering himself with an effort*): My dear sir, she was one of the finest women you ever saw in the whole course of your life! (*Aside:*) It's murder! By all the furies, it's murder. Who was she? What could have induced us to do it?

BLOGG: Was she dead?

FOGGERTY: Dead, but still warm. (*Aside:*) This is appalling! (*Aloud:*) And how – how do you think this unhappy lady met her miserable fate?

BLOGG (*after a pause*): Pound and a 'arf o' arsenic?

FOGGERTY: Very near a pound and a half of arsenic – not quite, but very nearly – purchased in small doses for the ostensible purpose of killing rats, and administered to her by – whom do you suppose? (*Waits anxiously for* BLOGG*'s reply.*)

BLOGG: Oh, Walkinshaw, of course?

FOGGERTY (*relieved and shaking his hand*): My dear fellow, I did you an injustice. I took you for an ass. Allow me to apologise – you are one of the sharpest men I have met for a long time. Of course it was administered by Walkinshaw. And how do you suppose that fiend in human form contrived to administer this deleterious mineral to his ill-fated victim?

BLOGG (*after a pause*): Apple pudden?

FOGGERTY: You are quite right; it *was* in an apple pudding – a large apple pudding, the apples having been previously pared and cut in quarters and the cores extracted. Now the question is – and a very important question it is – how far am I implicated?

BLOGG: Ah! that is the question.

FOGGERTY: True, I assisted him in disposing of the body. True, I went even so far as to dig the hole that was to receive it. But then the question arises – how did I come to do it? How came I to be there at all?

BLOGG: Oh! you was a walkin' in your sleep.

FOGGERTY: I was in a state of the profoundest somnambulistic unconsciousness. I give you my untarnished word of honour I was snoring heavily during the whole transaction. As for the lady – who do you think she was? Of all unlikely people on the face of this earth, who do you suppose that beautiful but unhappy lady was?

BLOGG (*pleasantly*): Suppose we say his aunt – his aunt Sarah?

FOGGERTY: It was his admirable aunt Sarah – as excellent and blameless a lady as ever stepped, and, I assure you, a first-rate aunt – a really capital aunt. In point of fact, she had but one fault in her composition, and I needn't tell you what that was.

BLOGG (*after a pause*): Drink?

FOGGERTY: Her passion for alcoholic stimulants was that lovely but deeply injured lady's bane. Beginning with small and comparatively harmless drams, the detestable habit gradually grew upon her, and she got from one thing to another (for I am anxious to omit nothing, however insignificant, from my confession), until at last she degenerated into a monomaniacal dipsomaniac.

BLOGG: Lor'!

FOGGERTY: Walkinshaw, one of the most exemplary nephews in the world, really couldn't stand it any longer. His credit as a gentleman, his position in society, his very means of livelihood were all affected by the disreputable habits of this abominable old lady – one of the finest women you ever saw. One day he made a large apple pudding and flavoured it with nearly a pound and a half of arsenic, and I, in one of those fits of somnambulistic unconsciousness to which I have been subject from infancy, dug a hole to receive the body, snoring heavily the whole time. (*Aside:*) There, I have done it now. What *have* I said? Oh, Walkinshaw, Walkinshaw, if I only had my fingers round your throat at this moment, justice would be baulked of her victim.

(*Enter* WALKINSHAW *hurriedly, in greatcoat and rug, and carrying luggage.*)

WALKINSHAW (*in great distress*): She has found me out. She is after me. I can just catch the nine forty-five; but I have not a moment to lose.

FOGGERTY (*seizing him*): Stop, scoundrel! Miscreant! Stop!

WALKINSHAW: What do you mean? Let me go! I'm bolting!

FOGGERTY: Bolting, are you? Not while I have the strength of twenty men, as I have now. (*Struggling desperately with him.*)

BLOGG (*to* WALKINSHAW): You had best stop. Do what the poor gentleman tells you. Don't contrairy him.

WALKINSHAW: Stop! I can't stop! Let me go! Don't shake me! You're always rumpling me!

FOGGERTY (*furiously*): Rumple you! I'll rumple you! (*Shakes him violently,* WALKINSHAW *quite helpless in his hands.*)

WALKINSHAW (*breathless*): Pray don't – let me go!

BLOGG: Better let the poor gentleman rumple you, if he wants to.

FOGGERTY: Abandon all hope of escape! Your diabolical treatment of that amiable and deeply-injured lady will soon be blown to the four corners of the earth. (*Shakes him violently.*)

WALKINSHAW: I didn't treat her handsomely, I admit. But you treated her just as badly as I did.

FOGGERTY (*remorsefully*): I did. I know it. Guilty wretch that I am! But who led me into it? Who used his diabolical power over me to compel me to act as his accomplice? Oh, I could throttle you! (*Shakes him.*)

WALKINSHAW (*faintly*): If you will kindly desist for a moment, perhaps I could answer you.

BLOGG (*aside to* WALKINSHAW): Don't contrairy him, sir. Best let the poor gentleman throttle you if he wants to. It's the only way.

WALKINSHAW: Hush! She is coming! She is after me! Hide me – hide me! She follows me wherever I go.

FOGGERTY (*flinging him off*): The conscience-stricken coward is haunted by the imaginary presence of his miserable victim!

WALKINSHAW (*very faintly, and all of a heap*): Don't quite understand.

FOGGERTY: Understand that I have confessed everything. Your beautiful but ill-fated aunt Sarah—

WALKINSHAW: I haven't got an aunt Sarah.

FOGGERTY: Her unfortunate passion for drink – the apple pudding – the arsenic – her agonising death – the blood-stained sack and its ghastly tenant – the midnight grave!

WALKINSHAW (*very faintly*): Some mistake somewhere.

FOGGERTY: Officer, seize him!

BLOGG: But—

FOGGERTY: Seize him, I say.

BLOGG (*going to* WALKINSHAW, *who is all of a heap against the table*): Werry sorry, sir! But the poor gentleman mustn't be contrairied. (*Seizes* WALKINSHAW.)

WALKINSHAW (*very limp and helpless*): Don't *you* rumple me!

(BLOGG *sits at table with* WALKINSHAW, *a helpless lump in his lap. Enter* MALVINA, *hurriedly.*)

MALVINA: He came this way. (*Sees* WALKINSHAW *in* BLOGG*'s lap.*) Oh, here he is – now – now I have got you.

(WALKINSHAW *stares helplessly at her like an idiotic baby.*)

FOGGERTY (*to* MALVINA): Don't touch him – he is a murderer!

MALVINA: A murderer! (*Recoiling towards* FOGGERTY.)

(BLOGG *rises, places* WALKINSHAW *on a chair like a helpless Guy Fawkes.*)

BLOGG (*aside to* MALVINA, *who is reclining in* FOGGERTY*'s arms*): Take my advice, and don't you go too near him, miss. He is a madman.

MALVINA: A madman! (*Recoiling from* FOGGERTY, *who for the first time understands that he is regarded as a lunatic, and assumes an expression of horror-struck surprise.*) A murderer and a madman! And woe is me, it is to such men as these that I have handed over my unsuspecting heart!

(*Enter* TALBOT.)

TALBOT (*aside to* BLOGG): We are quite ready to remove him; but I'll break it pleasantly to him. (*Aloud:*) My dear Foggerty, I'm extremely sorry to say that it is necessary to place you under restraint.

FOGGERTY: Under restraint! I see it all now. They take me for a madman. It only needed this to complete my misery.

BLOGG: Come along o' me. There's a cab at the door, and it'll be done as comfortable as possible.

FOGGERTY: Away!

(*Throwing* TALBOT *and* BLOGG *off.* TALBOT *falls helplessly into a chair;* BLOGG *goes off.*)

Matters have reached a crisis. There's only one thing to be done. I have Rebecca's pills in my pocket. One last appeal to her, and if that fails, I give in. (*Pours out a glass of water and swallows pill.*) Rebecca! Appear!

(*Hurried music.* REBECCA *appears through trap.*)

REBECCA (*impatiently*): Now, what do you want? I'm extremely busy, and this interruption is most annoying.

FOGGERTY: I won't detain you long. In my anxiety to appear equal to the intellectual pressure of the conversation, I've been led into making such preposterous statements that I run a very good chance of being hanged first and confined in a lunatic asylum afterwards.

REBECCA: Really, this doesn't concern me. I've nothing to do with it. My guardianship is Spiffed out.

FOGGERTY: Yes, I know it's Spiffed out; but you're an extremely intelligent and accomplished young person – don't you think if you made an effort you could Spiff it in again?

REBECCA: Out of the question. I should have to admit that I made a mistake, and I should be at once relegated to the back rows, among the stout ones, and never allowed to dance, even in a quartet, and lately I've been dancing solo.

FOGGERTY: But—

REBECCA: I've nothing more to say; your situation doesn't concern me in any way. I beg I may not be interrupted again. (*On trap, stamps her foot and says, 'Go' – she descends through trap.*)

FOGGERTY: Stop!

REBECCA (*half down trap*): What *do* you want? (*Remains halfway down trap.*)

FOGGERTY: Allow me to remind you that I've forty-seven pills left, and I can call you up forty-seven times if I please. I don't want to make myself unpleasant to a lady, but if you're not civil, I'll give you a time of it.

REBECCA (*rising through trap again*): Well, be quick. What is it?

FOGGERTY: Let's understand one another. When I took the draught all the consequences of my having known Spiff were obliterated.

REBECCA: Utterly.

FOGGERTY: But if I had never known Spiff I should never have got into a difficulty on account of Spiff, and if I had never got into that difficulty I should never have applied to you to get me out of it, and if I had never applied to you to get me out of it you would never have given me that infernal draught, which has been the cause of all the miseries with which I'm threatened.

REBECCA: Dear me, I never thought of that.

FOGGERTY: In point of fact, I've been saddled with consequences from which, according to the terms of my contract, I ought to have been entirely free.

REBECCA: It certainly seems so. I'm very sorry.

FOGGERTY: Now all this comes of hurrying your work. If you'd do a little less bedevilment and do it well you'd make a better job of it in the end.

REBECCA: It's not bedevilment. I'm a good fairy.

FOGGERTY: Good, but stupid.

REBECCA: Good, but stupid. I hope you won't mention this?

FOGGERTY: That depends upon yourself. You've got me into this fix, and you must get me out of it. Restore matters to their original condition, barring Spiff, whom I won't hear of at any price, and we'll say no more about it.

REBECCA: Very good, I'll do it; but mind, it must never be known that I 'tried back', or I should get into a terrible scrape. Are you ready for the change?

FOGGERTY: Quite ready.

REBECCA: Then 'go'.

(*Waves wand. Slow music. Scene suddenly changes to scene of Act I, daylight. All the* FAIRIES *enter at the back and group until the end.* TALBOT, MALVINA *and* WALKINSHAW *gradually revive from their swoon.* MALVINA *goes to* WALKINSHAW.)

MALVINA: Walkinshaw! My own!

WALKINSHAW: Malvina! (*Embraces.*)

(*Enter* JENNY, *followed by* LOTTIE *and* TOTTIE *in dresses of Act I, then* UNCLE FOGLE, AUNT BOGLE, WALKER *and* BALKER, *all in dresses of Act I, with favours.* JENNY *rushes to* FOGGERTY.)

JENNY: Frederick! My own.

FOGGERTY: Jenny! (*Embraces.*)

TALBOT: Now then – come along – the carriages have been waiting ever so long, and the clergyman is getting cold. Uncle Fogle, take Aunt Bogle; Walker, take Lottie; Balker, take Tottie.

JENNY: Frederick! In ten minutes we shall be made one. Tell me once more that you have never, never loved before!

FOGGERTY: Never – wouldn't dream of such a thing! It's all right; it's all over – it's past – gone – Spiffed out for ever!

JENNY: What's spiffed out?

FOGGERTY: Medical men – madhouse – breach of promise – execution – murdered aunt Sarah! All gone!

WALKINSHAW: What's the man talking about?

FOGGERTY (*suddenly serious*): Walkinshaw, you did *not* murder your aunt Sarah?

WALKINSHAW: Never!

TALBOT: Oh, too absurd! Ha! ha! ha!

ALL: Ha! ha! ha!

FOGGERTY: Walkinshaw, you are going to be married to Malvina. If, in the fullness of time, Heaven should ever bless you with a little aunt Sarah, swear that that admirable woman's life shall be as sacred as your own!

WALKINSHAW: Before Heaven, I swear it.

FOGGERTY: I knew it! God bless you, Walkinshaw.

ALL: Ha! ha! ha!

FOGGERTY: And, Jenny – dear Jenny – you won't marry Walkinshaw, but, on the contrary, you'll marry me, and Walkinshaw will marry Malvina; she has an excellent constitution. And Walker, Balker, Lottie, Tottie, Fogle, Bogle, you'll all marry each other!

(*All laugh.*)

And I declare I'm so happy I don't know whether to
laugh or to cry.

(*All laughing.*)

Which shall it be? Oh, well, better be unanimous.
Ha! ha! ha! ha! ha!
ALL: Ha! ha! ha! ha! ha!

(*They pair off.* FOGGERTY *with* JENNY, WALKINSHAW *with*
MALVINA, WALKER *with* LOTTIE, BALKER *with* TOTTIE,
UNCLE FOGLE *with* AUNT BOGLE, *and move towards
entrance, laughing heartily. Scene opens at back during this.*
FAIRIES *enter, laughing heartily, and waving wands.* REBECCA
*ascends on stool at back, also laughing. Red fire.**)

CURTAIN

NOTE ON THE TEXT

The text of this edition is based on that printed in Gilbert's *Original Plays: Third Series* (London: Chatto & Windus, 1895, 'OP3'), which appears to reflect the latest state of the script by the end of its original run. A pre-production copy of the script ('PPC'), apparently used during rehearsals, held in the British Library (Add MS 49314) has also been consulted; this has provided the original opening scene for Act II and an important correction to the body of the text. As was conventional at the time, many of the stage directions were given after the action they direct; in this edition they have been moved up to their conventional position in front of the directed action. In some cases, spelling and punctuation have been silently corrected to make the text more appealing to the modern reader.

NOTES

1   *On a banni… Fancy*: Quoted in the programme for the original production of *Foggerty's Fairy* at the Criterion Theatre. The lines are from Voltaire's verse *conte philosophique* '*Ce qui plait aux dames*' (1764), which derives from the 'Wife of Bath's Tale' in Chaucer's *Canterbury Tales*.

7   *favours*: In the mid-Victorian period, a wedding guest would wear on their coat or dress a 'favour' – that is, a rosette or knot of ribbons (later flowers).

15   *actions for breach of promise*: A promise to marry was considered a legal contract, and a suit for breach of promise could be brought for breaking that contract. The law was changed in 1970 in England and Wales, effectively abolishing breach of promise.

19   *clarionet*: A now obsolete version of 'clarinet'.

21   *tutelary*: That is, serving as a protector or guardian. The rhyming phrase 'tutelary fairy' bring to mind the Gilbert and Sullivan opera *Iolanthe*, which Gilbert was writing at the time *Foggerty's Fairy* was performed:

> Your badinage so airy,
> Your manner arbitrary,
> Are out of place
> When face to face
> With an influential Fairy.

25   *jumping through a window*: Harlequin, the nominal hero of the harlequinade of Victorian pantomime, and traditionally shown as Columbine's paramour, was given to acrobatic antics including leaping through windows.

25   *Vampire*: The so-called 'vampire trap' was a kind of trapdoor, invented for James Robinson Planché's Gothic chiller *The Vampire* (1820), which allowed figures to seem to pass through walls or floors.

26   *human ward in fairy chancery*: A ward in Chancery was a minor under the protection of the Court of Chancery.

31   *Collaring him*: Seizing him by the collar, as if to arrest him. In PPC, here and later (see following note), it is specified that Miss Spiff hooks her umbrella under Foggerty's collar.

33 *I'm lost*: PPC here has the following stage direction for Foggerty: '*Takes Spiff's umbrella and hooks it into his collar.*'

37 *A handsomely… trap in stage*: PPC has a longer opening scene here instead of Rebecca's monologue: see Appendix.

38 *Here we are again*: This was the pantomime clown's traditional greeting to the audience at the start of the harlequinade.

41 *spiffed out*: That is, done up, smartened up.

41 *Spiffed in*: OP3 has 'Spiffed out', but this is an error; the correct version is shown in PPC.

49 *Themis*: In Greek mythology, Themis, the second wife of Zeus, is the personification of justice and fairness.

50 *my action*: That is, legal action for breach of promise.

50 *two-pair-back*: That is, a room at the back of the house on the second floor.

50 *the nonce*: The present.

66 *Commission*: A private patient required a medical certificate signed by two physicians, surgeons or apothecaries in order to be committed to an asylum.

71 *Commission de lunatico*: A commission *de lunatico inquirendo* was an official inquiry into the mental state of a patient.

76 *The worm in the bud*: A borrowing from Shakespeare's *Twelfth Night* (Act II, scene 4): 'But let concealment, like a worm i' the bud, feed on her damask cheek.'

76 *Make it pounds, do*: Before British currency was decimalised in 1971, one pound was composed of 20 shillings, and one guinea was 21 shillings.

97 *Red fire*: A theatrical effect evoking magical spirits, especially associated with pantomimes.

APPENDIX

The Original Act II Opening

Five or six FAIRIES *are seated about the room – in unconventional attitudes – some knitting, others hemming 'tacks'; one or two are reading newspapers and books.*

Enter FAIRY REBECCA *through trap, which works awkwardly.*

REBECCA (*to cellar men under the stage*): Now do be careful – don't jerk so. (*To* FAIRIES*:*) Any sign of his waking?

ROSELEAF: No, my dear. He's left off snoring, and that's a blessing. But he's fast asleep.

REBECCA: Well, I've an appointment at a Transformation in half an hour. There's nothing for it but to wake him.

DEWDROP: I'm glad of it. I'm getting rather tired of watching over his slumbers, and that's the truth. It's as bad as night nursing, and not half so well paid.

REBECCA: Ah! A Fairy's life is not a bed of roses, my dear! I don't believe there's one of us who wouldn't be only too glad to change places with the seediest mortal going. Dear me, when I see a crooked old charwoman scrubbing on her knees in a damp scullery and grumbling at her hard lot, I feel inclined to say to her, 'Ah! it's all very well, old lady, but if you want to know what real hard work and discomfort are, just try Fairyland on a cold night.'

ALL (*shuddering*): Ugh!

REBECCA: To have to pass one's life in draughty Transformation Scenes, standing on one leg for half an hour at a stretch, is bad enough, to say nothing of being shot through the earth on a dusty trap, like coals; but when it comes to Fairy Revels of a couple of dozen middle-aged women dancing with each other (*imitating ballet action*) – 'la de da – la de da' – and not a man within miles, why, *I* say, give me a Camden Town party of the cut-orange-and-ham-sandwich order for choice! But come, let's wake Mr Foggerty.

DEWDROP: What shall we sing?

REBECCA: Oh, the old thing I suppose, 'Wake, mortal, wake'.

DEWDROP: But it's so hackneyed, and the words are so stupid.

REBECCA: Bless you, he won't hear them. It'll do as well as anything else.

ROSELEAF: Let's see, how does it go?

REBECCA: Don't you remember? (*Humming a few bars of the air:*) 'La la la la.'

ROSELEAF: Of course, I remember now.

REBECCA: But come, girls – group yourselves – for goodness' sake don't let him see you *en deshabille*. Dewdrop, you go there; Cowslip, pose yourself with Bluebell – arm higher – no, no – round the elbow – that's it – keep that – very good – now then (*giving them the time during symphony*) – one, two, three, four...

REBECCA *and* FAIRIES (*singing*):
    Wake, mortal, wake,
        Thy magic dream is o'er –
    Thy couch forsake –
        To earth return once more –
    So ope thine eyes –
        And wonders thou shalt see,
    A great surprise
        Is now in store for thee.

(They wave their wands over him as they sing. During this song FOGGERTY *yawns, stretches himself, then turns over and goes to sleep again. As the song proceeds he again yawns, rubs his eyes and gradually awakes, as if from a heavy sleep. All the* FAIRIES *twirl off and disappear, except* REBECCA.*)*